AROUND THE BEND

A NOVEL

BRITNEY KING

WWW.BRITNEYKING.COM

COPYRIGHT

Hot Banana Press

Cover Design by Britney King

Cover Image by Mandy Hollis

Copy Editing by Literary Agent Rogena Mitchell-Jones

Proofread by Proofreading by the Page

First Edition: 2014

ISBN: 978-0-9892184-4-3 (Paperback)

ISBN: 978-0-9892184-5-0 (All E-Books)

britneyking.com

To Jeremy, I miss you every day.
And to everyone who has ever loved someone through the pain.

AROUND THE BEND

BRITNEY KING

CHAPTER ONE

Never assume things can't get worse. If you were to ask her what she'd learned over the past year, that's exactly what Jessica Clemens would have said. Well, that and more, but at the very least, this would, first and foremost, be it.

Things can always, always get worse.

Take for example the afternoon Jess was lounging in her sitting room pondering the shit-storm that had become her life when he, and by he, I'm referring to her husband Spencer, walked out of his closet, bags in hand.

This is how it all began. Her coming undone.

Truth be told, it began long before this. But that's the funny thing about stories, isn't it? It's hard to tell where the beginning and end are.

Now, had Jess been paying attention or hell, even been sober, she might have seen this coming. Alas, she did not. And so, things did get worse from that moment on. Much, much worse.

3

That bright and cool spring afternoon, Spencer stood in front of his wife with a certain somber look on his face. It could have been remorse, she wasn't sure, for she was too high to tell the difference. The truth was, he had given Jess that look almost daily over the previous six months—so much so, she wasn't sure if it was her or if it had simply become his natural expression.

She glanced at him, down at his bags, and then cocked her brow. "I didn't know you had a trip this week," she said as she reached for her tumbler of vodka.

Spencer dropped the luggage and sat down on the footstool opposite her. "I'm fairly certain I told you..." He eyed her with pity, or perhaps anger, she couldn't gauge which. He started to speak again, but then paused before continuing. "You're looking a bit better today. And you're up." He smiled. "That's good news, isn't it?" He didn't wait for her to answer. "At any rate, I'm glad because we need to talk. This trip is going to be a bit of an extended one."

Jess eyed his bags again. "I can see that," she slurred tipping the glass in his direction.

He lowered his voice and spoke clearly, calmly—as though he were trying to talk her down from a ledge that she wasn't even aware she was hanging from. Jess knew better. She'd already fallen. "Jessica. Please. I know these past few months have been hard for you with the accident and all... and well, now this. But you need to understand that I'm not leaving for good. It'll only be a few weeks or so—a month max."

Had she been sober, she might have had the right mind to be angry, or to be hurt, or even devastated as she rightfully should've been. Instead, she found she was indifferent.

"Well... sayonara. And here's to you." She raised her glass, then threw her head back and laughed. The man she'd loved for the past decade was, for the most part, walking out on

4

her at a time when she clearly, really, *really* needed him, and she found it funny. That's how much trouble she was in. And Jess didn't even have the good sense to know it.

"Jessica." He reached for the tumbler, slid it forcefully from her hand, and placed it on the table. He stared at the glass as though he couldn't stand to look at her. "I need you to listen to what I'm trying to say here." He spoke, and then waited to ensure he had her attention before he continued. "I spoke to Addison at the agency a few moments ago. She's going to audit our staff and see what is needed in my absence. To start with, she's going to send someone over ASAP to help you get around a little more while I'm away..."

Jess scoffed. "You don't think we have enough help?"

"I don't want you to worry about anything." He took a deep breath and let it out. "Anyhow, about the children..."

"The children?" She interrupted defensively, even though the probability was low at that moment that she even had the prudence to consider the fact that they even had children. *That she had children.* That this would affect them.

"Yes, Jessica. Our children. Jonathan and Catherine..." He looked at the glass and back at her. "You do remember them, right?"

Jess sighed, picked up the glass, and finished it off. But she didn't take her eyes off his. Jess was a lot of things, but she wasn't dumb. She wouldn't admit defeat. "I'm not the one going on an extended vacation."

He raised his voice then. "This isn't a vacation, Jessica. This is business. And... quite frankly, I need to get away for a bit. I can't just sit around here twiddling my thumbs while my wife deteriorates into nothingness. Once again, you're not getting it." He paused, running his hands through his hair. Jess watched as his fingers slid slowly through his dark brown hair, which she'd always thought reminded her of smooth, silky chocolate, and wondered just how long it had been since she'd done the same.

"We've been over and over this… I'm not sure how else to say it. I need to give you some space to handle things on your own… Ever since the accident, well, I think you've forgotten who you are. While I'm gone, I want you to focus on getting back to your old self. I figure the only way you'll do that is if I force your hand."

Jess glanced toward the door and back at her husband. "So what are you waiting for then?"

She watched as he took one last look at her, stood, and walked out, all straight-backed and righteous. But all she could think about at that moment was what the women at the Ladies Who Lunch event would say the following day and every day after that. Because Jess, as drunk and high as she might have been, realized more than her husband did that afternoon. He was never coming back. Not really, anyway.

～

CHAPTER TWO

SIX MONTHS EARLIER

J ess had been looking forward to this dinner all week. Mostly because she knew Spencer was excited about it, and these days, he rarely seemed excited about anything. *The fact that he had even asked her to accompany him to a business dinner had surely been a good sign, hadn't it?* Her husband had seemed off for the past few months, and while she knew his work had been particularly stressful, she couldn't help but feel that some part of it was because of her.

Jess heard him call for her from somewhere downstairs. She checked herself in the mirror, fastened her diamond earring in place, and slipped on her new Jimmy Choos. As she rounded the corner to the children's wing of the house, she heard them arguing as one of the nannies attempted to shush them. Jess opened the door and braced herself against the doorframe as Catherine came barreling toward her.

"Mommy?" Her daughter eyed her up and down. "Are you and Daddy going on a date?"

"I already told you that, genius," Jonathan piped in.

"Jonathan," Jess chided. Her son, at eleven, was growing moodier by the day, and she sensed it was at least equal to his father's growing unhappiness. *How was it kids never missed a thing, she wondered.* Not only did they not miss it, but they also soaked it up like the little sponges they were. She knelt down and smoothed her daughter's bangs back from her eyes, but her gaze was fixed on her son. "We are, sweetheart. But I'll make sure to tiptoe in and kiss you goodnight just as soon as we get home." Her daughter, Catherine, or Kit Cat, as they'd taken to calling her, leaped forward into her arms. "I'll miss you, Mommy." Jess kissed the tip of her nose then hugged her close, inhaling the scent of her still damp hair. Jess loved those moments when she still got the occasional glimpse of the toddler her now seven-year-old had once been.

She pulled back and looked at her son who seemed to have already forgotten her presence, his attention now turned back to his iPad. "Jonathan, did you have your shower, too?" She looked to Serena, the children's nanny, and back at her son, knowing the answer before either of them answered.

"I don't like showers," he stated without looking up.

Jess walked over and slid the device from his hands. He looked up, none too pleased. "That isn't what I asked. I asked if you'd had one. Now, run along and then Serena will let you have this back when you're washed up."

He threw up his hands dramatically and let out a loud sigh. "Fine."

Jess grabbed his tiny wrist. She pulled him to her, or as close as he would let her, and ran her fingers through his shaggy, light brown hair, the same shade as hers. She took his chin between her fingers and gently turned his face to face her. He feigned annoyance, but Jess sensed that at least a small part of him still needed this, even if he wanted to be too big to admit it. "I love you so, so, so much, you know that, right?" His green eyes flickered with a hint of something she'd remembered seeing all those endless nights when she had held him, rocking him, praying he might sleep. It wasn't that her son had been a difficult baby—he never cried, but he never slept either. Being that he was her first, she hadn't yet the good sense, or the confidence to know he might be okay, if she just let him be. *'He doesn't need to be held all of the time, Jessica,'* Spencer would say. *'You don't have to entertain him, you know,'* he would scold. *'You're creating a monster. That's what we have nannies for. Do you think we pay these people for nothing?'* But Jessica didn't care. She was his mother. This was what she wanted. She wanted to do things differently than either of their parents had, she'd said. And maybe that defiance was the fracture that started a much larger break in her marriage —the break she was working to fix, and tonight, she was sure Spencer's insistence that she attend dinner with him was just one small step in the right direction.

Jess let Jonathan go before she bent down and kissed her kids once more. She stopped in the doorway, turning back. "Serena, please see to it that the children have hair appointments set up."

The nanny nodded and Jess smiled just a little.

Later, she would remember, while it was an insignificant thing to say at the time, it would be the last thing she would say for quite a while that would make her feel like she was actually someone's mother.

"YOU DID REALLY GOOD IN THERE," SPENCER SAID, HOLDING the passenger door of their Range Rover open for her.

Jess laughed, pausing to gaze up at the stars. They were having an Indian summer and it was still warm, even at nearly midnight. "Yeah, I guess I've still got it, huh." She eyed her husband and noticed the way he looked at her—as though maybe it was the first time he was really seeing her in a very long time. She cocked her head. "Are you sure you're all right to drive?"

He pursed his lips and Jess suddenly remembered how her husband hated being questioned. "I'm fine. I just had a few drinks, but that was hours ago."

She nodded and climbed in. "Well, I'm still feeling tipsy, and I only had one of Jim's cocktails," Jess added for good measure. *Things were going so well. She should have known better and chosen her words a little more carefully.*

Jess watched her husband go around and climb into the driver's seat. He pulled his phone from his suit pocket, stared at the screen, and frowned.

"Everything okay?"

He placed the phone on the center console, looked over at her, and sighed as he turned the key in the ignition. "Just work stuff. Nothing that would be of concern to you." He smiled slightly and put the SUV in reverse.

Jess shifted in her seat and stared out at the darkness of the night as they pulled out of the winery and onto the two-lane country road. She had always liked it out here. It was so dark, so peaceful. And while she tried to focus on her surroundings versus the sting of her husband's words, it was ultimately the sting that won out. The familiar knot in her chest tightened. *Nothing that would concern her, she thought. Nothing that would concern her. Of course. And why should it?* It wasn't as though the work he had been discussing hadn't been the business her family had built over three generations. How could it possibly *not* concern her? This issue had also contributed to the distance between them, Jess had decided. Spencer was trying to do too much. Not only was he managing his family's international law firm, but he was attempting to take the reins in her family's affairs, as well. Jessica had tried to talk him out of it. Sure, her father wanted to retire and he'd had Spencer pegged as his replacement long ago, but they could always find someone else, Jess had assured him. She knew her father was impossible to please (for anyone but her) and that it took someone equally so, someone like her husband, to even remotely fit the bill, but still. There were other ways, she'd urged. And it certainly wasn't as though they needed the money. But then her father got ill and slowly started losing his memory, and then all at once, the man who had adored her all her life was gone. Well, not totally gone, as in dead, but he was a shell of the man he'd once been. These days, while she still visited as often as she could muster the courage, he barely remembered her at all. *Fast acting dementia, they'd called it.*

Spencer had been her rock through it all. He arranged everything and had most of the business assets transferred into her name as her mother wanted nothing whatsoever to do with any of it. Her brother, now living in Spain (or at least had been last she'd heard) and doing God knows what with his time and their family's money, only wanted his disbursement checks to keep rolling in, and in typical fashion, had signed off on any responsibility to the family business, so long as he could maintain the lifestyle he had always been accustomed to.

"Do you have plans tomorrow?"

"Work stuff. Why?"

"I thought we could go visit my dad. And take the kids. It's been a few weeks…"

He shook his head. "Jessica. I think you need to stop taking the children. Maybe stop going yourself for a while. I can see that it's wearing on you."

She did a double take, her mouth agape. "He's my father. I can't just pretend he's already gone."

"Isn't he, though?"

"Fuck you, Spence. That's a terrible thing to say."

Spencer exhaled and placed his hand on her arm. She pulled away. "That's not what I meant. It's just that you haven't been yourself lately. I think this whole situation is taking a toll on you, that's all. And I mean this with all due respect, but it's not as though he'll know whether you've come or gone anyway. I don't see what's so wrong with having the kids remember him as he was. That's how I want to remember him…"

Jess crossed her arms. "The 'situation' you're talking about is my father. Don't forget that. Maybe you don't understand loyalty, but I do."

The phone on the console lit up and rang so suddenly it startled Jess. Spencer eyed the phone and then grabbed it so abruptly that Jess watched as it slipped through his fingers in slow motion and fell onto the floorboard of the backseat.

"Shit… Can you grab that?" He pleaded, straining into the backseat fishing with his fingers.

She felt the car swerve slightly. "Spence!" He corrected the steering wheel. "Geez. Focus on the road… would you? I'll get the phone." She seethed. *Always the damned phone… No wonder they were having such a tough time with their son.*

"I've been waiting on that call," he uttered to her, or maybe just to himself, she wasn't sure.

She turned slightly looking in the backseat, noting that it was too dark to see anything. The ringing stopped and started again, and suddenly, she saw it behind the driver's seat, nudged up against the left passenger door. *It was after midnight. Who would call twice? Hopefully, it wasn't about the kids…*

"Do I need to pull over?"

Jess reached as far as she could. "No, I can get it," she said feeling the seatbelt refuse to give any further.

The phone stopped ringing and started again.

"Jessica!"

"I'm trying," she said unbuckling herself to allow herself to reach further.

Jess felt her fingertips graze the phone. "Ah. Got it," she announced proudly.

Jessica heard his sigh and then the screeching of tires. *The screeching of tires.* That would be the last thing she would hear for six whole days.

And afterward, in her dreams, for many more than she dared to admit.

JESSICA AWOKE TO HER BEST FRIEND WHISPERING HER NAME. She had thought she'd heard people in her room talking, but this was the first time she was actually able to force her eyes open.

"Jessica. Oh, Jess. Wake up. Come on," Addison whispered.

She felt the familiar sensation of her hand being rubbed. Jess willed her eyes open.

"Jessica! Oh, my God." Unable to keep her eyes open, the light was too bright, she watched Addison reach for something through the slits of her eyes.

Jess tried to ask what was happening, but she couldn't speak. Suddenly, she started to panic, unable to move her wrists.

Addison patted her arm and put her face close to hers so that their noses were almost touching. Jess couldn't focus.

"Jess. Jess! Calm down. Listen to me. I need you to stop fighting. You're okay." Addison glanced toward the door and then back at her. "Don't worry… They're coming."

Who is coming, she wondered.

She could see Addison mouthing the words, but Jess

wasn't sure she could hear them being said. *Something was wrong.*

And then, almost as though Jess had said it aloud even though she knew she hadn't—she couldn't, Addison answered, "You've been in an accident, sweetie. But you're all right. They're getting you all fixed up."

Jess's eyes trailed down to her wrist. She attempted to pull her arm toward her face to get a better look, but it wouldn't budge, and she couldn't see straight enough to put it all together.

"You're on a respirator. The restraints are a precaution. So you don't pull the tube out... We'll get them off just as soon as the doctors get in here."

Addison pressed the button again. And again. There was a buzzing sound and then a voice. "I need a doctor in here now!" She heard her friend shout.

An accident. *The screeching tires.* And with that, Jess faded back into the darkness.

CHAPTER THREE

The next time Jessica opened her eyes, she thought for a moment she might be dreaming. Or perhaps dead. *Maybe this is what heaven looks like, she considered for a second.* Jess eyed the flowers surrounding her bed. There was every kind of flower imaginable. She winced, knowing instantly that she wasn't dead as soon as she attempted to turn her head and the pain took over. And then Jessica remembered.

It is funny how there's always that moment just after you wake that nothing seems real, and you forget that something terrible has happened—when for the slightest period of time it seems that things are the same as *before.* In the moment right before you remember, all is peaceful and all is as it should be. It's fleeting but sometimes these certain moments last longer than others. Some days, it might be minutes, while others it's just a few seconds, when your mind tricks you and allows you this blissful reverie. *If only you could buy those minutes, Jess thinks.*

She tried to move her legs and attempted to use her arms to push upright, but the pain was too much to bear. She shifted slightly and her eye caught something in the corner.

Not something, she realized. Someone. Spencer. His eyes met hers and he looked relieved. She wanted to speak, but simply stared instead. Seconds passed, maybe minutes, before he set his laptop down and walked to her.

"How do you feel?" he whispered.

She shifted her gaze toward the flowers and nods at the pitcher of water.

Spencer reached for a cup at her bedside, placed the straw between her lips, and watched her gulp down as much as she could before he pulled it away. "Not too much," he said. "We don't want you getting sick again."

Jess frowned. "How long have I been here?"

"Fourteen days."

Fourteen days? Jess considered. That's two whole weeks. "Where are the kids? *How* are the kids?"

Spencer pursed his lips. "They're fine. Your mother is with them. They know about the accident... that you're hurt and have had a few surgeries but that you're in here getting all fixed up and that you'll be home with them soon."

"How many surgeries?"

Spencer looked away as he spoke. "Three so far. But you're doing great. The doctors are very pleased with how things are coming along."

Jess felt the tears sting at the corner of her eyelids. She knew her husband's tone and what his unwillingness to look her in the eye meant.

"Spencer?" He turned and Jess saw that fake smile she knew so well. "How long am I going to be here?"

His smile faded slowly at first and then all at once. "I don't know." He sighed.

And finally, they were getting somewhere, Jess thought.

~

THE FOLLOWING WEEK WENT BY IN A FOGGY HAZE WITH MORE flower deliveries and more nurses than she could count. There were a few visitors here and there. Addison was there every day, sometimes twice a day, as was Jess's mother. Spencer came in the evenings, and this became how Jess marked her day, based upon who was there and when.

The days in the hospital that immediately followed the accident seemed to drag on as the pain increased ever more with each passing day. Jessica tried to stay on top of the pain, just as the doctors advised, but she didn't like the way the drugs made her feel. Without them though, she found the nagging pain she endured was more than she could bear. The doctors told her she needed to accept that it was going to take her body some time to heal and that she needed the narcotics to help facilitate the process. But Jess found it to be a double-edged sword as she was either in pain—or out of it all together, and she couldn't be sure which was the lesser evil.

In turn, she found that sleep was the only safe place, so she did a lot of it, and when she couldn't slip into the oblivion she so desperately craved, she pretended to. At first, Jess loved having visitors come. It broke up the day and it was nice to have company for a little while. But as the days wore on, and the reality that Jess could do almost nothing to care for herself, the visitors only served as a reminder of how bad things for her actually were. *They* left. *They* went back to their lives. *They* exited the hospital. *They* were able to see the blue expanse of the sky and the leaves on the trees. All Jess saw were four white walls, pity, and flowers—who, like her, had been plucked from their lives and set upon a different path altogether.

The more this new path was revealed to her, the more Jess found herself pressing the button attached to the automatic pump that delivered her pain meds. She began sleeping more, or at least pretending to, when Addison, her mother, or Spencer would visit, and before long, the visits slowed some. She still had yet to see her children, but that was because ICU didn't allow children under the age of twelve to visit. She'd argued once with Spencer over this, knowing that surely a few strings could be pulled, but he refused, saying it was best that they see her when she was feeling a bit more like herself. Jessica hadn't the strength to press the matter any further, for it was enough to try to make the pain go away. It wasn't long before the lines became blurred, and she couldn't determine which was worse—the physical pain she felt each day or the emotional pain of what she had become.

SOMETIME IN THE THIRD WEEK OF HER STAY, THERE WAS A fourth surgery, which would place pins in her right leg. Jess remembers wondering in the seconds before they put her under if she might be better off not waking up.

Later, when Jess awoke, she felt the slightest bit of disappointment followed by an incredible amount of guilt. She quickly did a double take as she took in the two tiny faces peering back at her. Jess felt someone squeeze her hand. She shifted her gaze downward. *Addison.*

"Hey, there." Addison grinned. "We've got two people here who are very anxious to see their mom."

Jess studied her children's faces. *They looked so grown up.*

She reached up and touched her daughter's face. Then she let her gaze shift to Jonathan, unable to ignore the worried expression he wore. She smiled. "Hey, you guys, wanna see how they fixed up my leg? They say I have so much metal in me that I'm practically a robot now."

Catherine's eyes widened. Her face had gone pale. "There's blood on the sheet."

A booming voice interrupted her. "Maybe some other time, Jessica. We can't stay too long."

Jess turned to see Addison's husband William standing above her bed and suddenly felt self-conscious.

Addison stepped forward, placed her arms on Catherine's shoulders, and pulled her close. *What Jess wouldn't have given at that moment to be the one comforting her daughter.*

"We sent Spencer to lunch," Addison said giving Jess a knowing look. "I had William help me get these guys up here, but, unfortunately, he's right—they won't let us stay very long."

Jess swallowed.

"We made these for you, Mommy," Catherine said thrusting a stack of papers at her. Jess attempted to pick them up, but her hands weren't cooperating. All at once, it was as though her arms were made of spaghetti. There seemed to be a disconnection from what Jessica wanted to happen and what was actually happening. William took the papers from Catherine and held them up, one by one so that Jess could take them in. Jess couldn't help but notice the way her daughter beamed with pride as she described each drawing, and also the way that William carefully handled them, as though he were handling priceless pieces fit for a gallery. She took it all in, realizing then just how much she'd missed this. She missed her kids. She missed her husband, her family, and her friends. She missed the little things that made up the whole of her life. She missed the thing that only a few weeks prior she'd so easily taken for granted.

Jonathan stepped forward interrupting her thoughts. He laid a notebook on top of her stomach. "I wrote this for you... I mean, I know you can't read it now... but maybe whenever we get to come back, I can read it to you." Jess looked into her son's big, bright eyes and found herself lost in them. Recently, he'd seemed so grown up, hell bent on proving that he no longer needed her. But looking at him now with so much unspoken anxiety written across his face, she knew better.

She smiled at her children, back at Addison, and finally at William, and she understood then that she had to do her very best to get back in the saddle and get home to them as soon as possible.

Jess wanted to tell them that, to reassure them that everything was going to be okay and that she was grateful for second chances to get it right. But, in that moment, a simple thank you was all she could manage.

SEVERAL DAYS FOLLOWING THE SURGERY, JESSICA WAS transferred to an inpatient rehabilitation hospital where she had been assured they were more equipped to handle the rehabilitation process. She had hoped to go home to recover, but her doctors, and especially her husband, insisted the rehabilitation hospital was a more logical alternative. Jess still wasn't able to sit upright for long periods of time due to a broken clavicle and broken ribs.

She had not been out of bed, or even able to use the restroom on her own since the accident. But the doctors and therapists assured her if she worked really hard, it was likely she could go home before Christmas. This was the only reason Jess had agreed to continue to take the pain meds despite the fact that they made her feel so out of it. The drugs took away the pain, sure, but they dulled other things, namely her senses. She was forgetful and foggy. She was either on top of the world or at rock bottom. They numbed the pain, but they also numbed her. But without the meds, the world was a less colorful, quieter place.

The children visited almost daily with their nanny, and

those visits were always the highlight of Jess's day. It was ironic, sad, and admittedly, a little funny how much Jessica's relationship with her children had changed since the accident.

Her family had always had help, but even still, she found herself so immersed in the nitty-gritty stuff, the day in and day out incessant decision making that life with children brings, she had a different perspective now that her sole focus had become herself and her recovery. She found joy in her kids again. She enjoyed hearing about their lives and their thoughts. Instead of the busy, rushed pace they all knew so well before the accident, now there seemed to be nothing *but* time. There was nowhere for her to go, and nothing to do, except the long, arduous process of learning to walk again, all the while, each step bringing her closer to the person she had once been. On one hand, she wanted to get back to being *that* girl. But there was also a part of her who wondered if the girl that she had been was truly as happy as nostalgia made her out to be—and whether now, in hindsight, if she wanted to go back to being that girl at all.

THE THERAPIST EYED HER. "I THINK IT'S TIME, JESSICA."

Her head pounded. Though this was their second, possibly third session, she sized the woman up as though she were seeing her for the first time. The therapist (this one for her mind, which they insisted was just as necessary as the others, much to her annoyance) was well dressed, short, and trim. Not exactly pretty, but not entirely unattractive either.

"Well, I disagree."

The woman, whose name Jess had again forgotten (which, among other things, she blamed on the pain meds) jotted something down on the tablet in her lap and then met her gaze head on. "When do you think a good time would be then?"

Jessica considered the question for a moment. "When I can walk," was the answer she offered up, although 'how about never' was what she really wanted to say.

"And why is that?"

Jess rubbed her temples. "Um... look Miss..."

"Mason."

"Right. Miss.... Mason. As you can probably see, I'm not feeling well, and I'd really rather not discuss any of this with you today, if it's all the same to you."

"This is a part of your recovery, Jessica. You know that counseling is a part of the deal here. And, as you probably know, the injuries you've sustained are not only physical in nature. Unless you're superwoman, and let's face it, none of us are, this has to have taken quite a toll on you."

Jess stared blankly until the woman shifted in her seat. "How are the children, Mrs. Clemens?"

Jess cocked her head. "My children are fine."

"That's great." The woman jotted something else down on her notepad. "I see them here occasionally. And I'm glad to hear they visit so often. It's good for all of you."

How would you know what's good for any of us? You don't know me. You don't know my family, Jess wanted to shout and might have had her head not felt so foggy.

"Miss..." Jessica blanked again before composing herself... "I really am very tired, and I have a full afternoon of *actual* therapy ahead of me, so if you'll just excuse yourself—seeing that I'm unable to show you out since I'm stuck in this chair and all, well, I would really appreciate it."

"Mason. It's Ms. Mason. And no, I'm sorry, but I will *not*... excuse myself." The woman glanced at her watch and then back at Jessica. "We have exactly forty-seven minutes left in our session. And I have a job that I'm obligated to do during those forty-seven minutes. So, if it's all the same to you, I will just sit right here."

Jessica tried to wipe the stunned look off her face, but was likely unsuccessful. For the first time in as long as she could remember, someone had actually told her no.

❧

Jess stared at her reflection in the mirror, scarcely recognizing the person staring back at her. Is this what Ms. Mason wanted? *OK. Fine,* she thought.

That relentless damned therapist, as Jessica had taken to calling her, had spent the entirety of their last session together badgering Jess about allowing her friends to visit. If this were what it would take to get that woman off her back, then this is exactly what Jessica would do, she finally decided. The woman had assured Jess that it would help in her recovery to have some normalcy returned to her day-to-day life. Support, the therapist had called it.

Jess would show her all right. She dialed Addison's cell.

Addison answered on the first ring.

Jessica didn't wait for her to say hello. She spoke breathlessly. "I'm going to need a party planner. The very best you've got."

Addison sighed, she was none too familiar with her friend's latest antics. "*You* need a party planner?"

"Yep."

"Jessica, you have your own staff... you have people you've always used. Why are you asking me?"

"Maybe I don't want the people I normally use. I mean... this situation is *hardly* normal. Wouldn't you say?" *The truth was Jess couldn't recall whom she normally used. Drugs will do that to a person, she thought.*

"OK, well, you got me there. What is it you need exactly?"

Jess grinned at her reflection in the mirror, suddenly satisfied with herself. "I'm going to host a luncheon like no other... *here*... in this place."

"Oh, good god," Addison said, exasperated. "You, Clemens... are trouble. And I have to admit—I really, really like it."

∾

CHAPTER FOUR

Jessica worked extra hard in the three weeks leading up to the luncheon to ensure that she would no longer have to use 'the chair.' Her dedication paid off as two days before the event, which she had so meticulously planned, she found herself able to get around reasonably well by utilizing a walker.

She poured hours into her therapy each day, and what remained leftover, she devoted to planning the best party possible. Because the Ladies Who Lunch, as they called themselves liked nothing if not a good party. The Ladies Who Lunch was an organization which had formed over fifty something years ago by women in the community who had both excessive amounts of time and money. Her Grandmother had been of the original founding members, then her mother, and now her. Once you were married off it was simply a society you found yourself a part of, if you were of a certain class. As of four weeks ago, there were two hundred and sixty-seven women who qualified and paid their dues (often literally) and these women convened for lunch twice a month. Jess knew exactly how many members the organiza-

tion contained because she held the title of VP for the organization as well as served as chairperson of the hospitality
committee. She was thus in charge of welcoming new
members and keeping the existing ones happy. Which as it
turns out was less hard than it might seem. You simply stuck
them on a committee and kept them busy, which was easy
until—as it usually is with any group of women, it wasn't.
But by the time the typical drama began they were under the
careful guidance of their own committee chair and for the
most part no longer Jess's problem. It was sufficed to say, the
Ladies Who Lunch had a committee for everything.

Jess had made a sizable donation to the rehabilitation
facility in order to reserve the dining room during lunch
hour. It was only later that she would realize this might not
have been the smartest plan. Having your fellow inmates (as
Jess called them) eat in their rooms, certainly didn't win one
any fans. Mostly because when you're confined to a place
that you don't want to be in, mealtime becomes the highlight
of your day and a reason to get 'out into the world' even if
that world is only as far as the dining room.

The morning of the luncheon, Jess had her regular girl,
the one she used for special occasions, come in and do her
hair and makeup. She had someone assist her in making sure
her dress was perfectly in place—a dress which she'd had her
stylist purchase and then take back to the seamstress, not
once but twice, as over the previous few weeks Jess watched
the numbers on the scale drop faster than she could keep up
with. No doubt, a side effect of the narcotics, which were
known to cause a loss of appetite. But this wasn't to be a
problem today as she had decided to skip her meds
completely.

At a quarter till eleven, Jess made her way down to the
dining room and was pleased to find that the event planner
Addison referred had outdone herself. The room had been

transformed from the ridiculous dining hall overfilled with ranch-style themed decor into a beautiful, elegant space. The pleather chairs had been replaced by antique crystal Chiavari chairs and the round tables had been covered in white linen. The fluorescent lighting had been turned off and was substituted with ornate chandeliers that hung over each table. Flowers lined the peripheral of the room as far as the eye could see. The place settings alone were exquisite, and the aroma coming from the kitchen actually made Jess giddy—for it had been a long time since food of any kind had appealed to her.

As the first few guests arrived, she found herself immersed in the commotion, and it appeared as though nothing at all had changed since the last luncheon she'd attended, a little more than a month ago.

It was sometime after appetizers, but before announcements, when Jess began to feel light headed. Although she'd consumed a fair amount of hors d'oeuvres, she hadn't had pain meds in almost twelve hours, and she was beginning to become aware that she might not make it through the three hour-long luncheon without having them. She began to feel anxious and irritable so she found herself a chair and tried to catch her bearings. But it wasn't long before the cold sweats started, and it only got worse from there. Jess remembered as the room swirled around her that her nemesis if she ever had one, Shannon McCain, called for a nurse. President of the organization for six years running, Shannon had once been a close friend of Jessica's.

Now the two barely spoke, and Jess saw her for what she was—a twig of a woman no one dared disagree with and whose upright stance and blonde bob, cut precisely, nary a hair out of place, only served to prove that she was all business. The truth was Shannon had had it out for Jess ever since the two disagreed over what became later known as the

'Christmas Bazaar Incident.' It should have been known that the number one rule of the Ladies Who Lunch was never, ever to disagree with Shanon McCain. To do so, and to do so publicly, would mean certain demise. Jessica had not given careful enough consideration to this unspoken rule, and so it had become classic and almost humorous the way Jess's former friend had so passive-aggressively made her life hell by vetoing and negating every move she'd made since.

As Jess pondered this predicament, a nurse appeared and asked a series of questions. Once the oversized woman determined that Jess had forgone her evening and morning medication, she simply shook her head and assured the gaggle of women corralled around Jess that this was the cause of the faintness and that she would return with the pills in a few moments. Jess felt relieved, suddenly less anxious, knowing she could soon look forward to the familiar metallic taste of the chalky pills sliding down the back of her throat. She considered that she shouldn't have been so stupid to skip the only thing that gave her comfort these days, and she realized then that the pills were not the enemy as once believed. As Jess took in the women surrounding her, her mind suddenly transformed their heads into vultures. *Vultures waiting to consume their prey, she thought.* One of them handed Jess a glass of water, which she downed in three gulps. Jess tried to focus on the hallway, listening for the nurses footsteps, thinking surely it shouldn't be taking this long to get four little pills, but she couldn't help noticing how the women eyed her, a mixture of pity, worry, and something else Jess couldn't place written across their faces. As she searched for something to say, the nurse returned with her medication, thankfully. She chewed the pills instead of swallowing them, desperation taking over as her name was announced. It was time to address the crowd.

She downed another glass of water and swallowed before

carefully standing and making her way to the front of the room. All eyes were on her. Although Jess would scarcely remember the speech she made that day, she would later recall that she did at least two things right. She thanked everyone for coming, and even though she likely slurred, she did manage to make it through every single item on the list of upcoming events and agenda items that someone (presumably Shannon) had handed her.

The Ladies Who Lunch gave a standing ovation as Jessica slowly, carefully, and painfully made her way to her seat along the side of the room. She took her seat, finally, which was no small feat, but just as soon as she was settled and the servers began serving, Jess felt someone tap her on the shoulder. She turned and saw Shannon flanked by a few members of the board. Jess did her best to keep a straight face as Brenda, Shannon's Girl Friday, did her bidding. "Is there somewhere around here that we could have a little privacy?"

Jess smiled and glanced around. She did her best to scoot her chair out to face the group of women. "This seems as good a place as any."

Shannon looked nervously at the women seated around the table before clearing her throat. "Yes. How rude of me... I know it must be hard for you to get around." Shannon glanced at the women by her side and then looked back down at Jess. "Anyway, about that... the ladies and I were talking it over, and we can see that you obviously have a lot going on here." She paused as she seemed to search for the right words even though Jess was pretty sure that she'd had them planned out for quite some time. "The board and I have decided that it's best if you step down from your role as VP."

Jess smiled. "Well, that's convenient."

"We feel it's necessary given the circumstances," Brenda chimed in.

Shannon continued. "We just think that you need a little

reprieve… some time to pull yourself together. I mean… it's certainly reasonable considering all that's happened—"

Jess cut her off. "Don't tell me what's reasonable. Look around. I *have* fulfilled my duties… considering." She felt her face grow hot as she recalled just how hard she'd worked to make today happen. She eyed each of the women one by one, as it became more and more clear that there would be no argument she could offer up to change their minds. They had already been made up. Jess swallowed hard. "This is bullshit and you all know it."

"It's really for the best Jessica."

Jess attempted to swallow the rage she felt building, but it didn't stay down. Instead, it consumed her. Everything she'd been through since the accident came bubbling up to the surface. She felt the burn in the back of her throat as her voice grew louder. "The hell it is! You want me out, and you're using my accident as a means to an end. You know, it's a really convenient way to spin the bullshit that regularly spews from your mouths." As she stood, her voice grew louder until all eyes in the room were on her.

"Jessica, this isn't the time or place," Shannon whispered in a vain attempt to silence her.

But this only added fuel to Jess's fire. She threw up her hands to signify just how wronged she was. "Here you are, 'oh, poor, pathetic Jessica,' let's relieve her of her duties so she can recover. Well, fuck you! I'm not one of your charity cases, Shannon. You *think* you can hide behind your Manolo Blahnik's and your fake smile… but you're crazy if you think you're kidding anyone, Mrs. McCain." Jess stepped forward and spoke slowly, making sure her voice lingered over every word she was about to say. "Everyone knows your husband spends more time with his flavor of the month than he does at home." An audible gasp filled the room, but Jess didn't let it detour her. She smoothed her dress. "Besides, you can't do this," her words slurred as she nearly lost her balance. "It takes a board vote to relieve a member of their duties."

Shannon chuckled slightly and stepped back, clearly caught off guard. "Like I said, this is clearly a conversation for another time."

While Jess pictured a righteous 'fuck you' exiting in her mind, her body, as it had done so frequently as of late, once again betrayed her. Instead, she doubled over and vomited the contents of her stomach all over her former friend's expensive shoes.

Needless to say, this would be the last time Jess would see any of the Ladies Who Lunch for quite a while. It's hard, *even* for women of their educational and economic stature, to know what to say to a cripple who can't control not only her body, but also her mouth. To them, it probably seemed just as easy to stay away. And just as Jess had predicted without saying a word in that first session with 'the relentless dammed therapist,' they did.

CHAPTER FIVE

SIX MONTHS LATER

EARLY SPRING

As Myles gathered the few belongings he possessed and carefully placed them in a duffle bag once issued to him by the Navy, he considered how little knowledge he had about his next assignment. Going in blind wasn't exactly his style. To his credit, he did know a few things. His new employer was some ultra-rich family (that much Google had told him), and the lady of the house had recently suffered some sort of injury, and he was told that her husband had left on an 'extended business trip.' He also knew (thanks to Google Maps) that the family owned a twenty-two acre estate that needed managing. Most importantly, he was informed that his most important task was to watch over 'The Missus'—whatever that meant, he hadn't a clue. He only surmised and based on his experience, it didn't sound good.

But it hardly mattered anyhow. Myles was certain that anything would be better than the current gig he'd held up until a few hours ago overseeing Old Man Thompson. His role over the previous two months had been to serve as a caretaker for the Thompson Estate. Caretaker, in this sense, was code for listen to Mr. Thompson complain, and berate his staff so that his adult children didn't have to.

Other than managing the man's bigotry, his secondary role had been to care for Mr. Thompson's four poodles, which Myles assessed, according to Thompson's meticulously well-documented regimen, had more needs than most humans he knew. While Myles wouldn't exactly say he wasn't an animal lover—he simply didn't understand owning something—dog or not, which had greater grooming needs than oneself.

He wasn't thrilled with the assignment, but he needed the work. More so, he needed to keep busy. But a few weeks later, his unspoken prayers were answered when out of nowhere, Myles found that he'd been abruptly reassigned.

He figured that the old man had decided he didn't show his dogs the appropriate degree of affection, nor did he agree with his dogmatism and perhaps had requested that Myles look elsewhere for employment. It certainly wouldn't have come as a complete surprise. Reassignment seemed to be the MO for him lately. But the old man seemed generally sad at the news he was leaving which was quite odd given the fact that the man never much liked him to begin with.

But, nonetheless, Myles found himself with a Greyhound ticket headed south. Three days earlier a woman by the name of Addison Hartman from the agency that had placed him, phoned with an unexpected offer. She'd informed Myles that she had what she called 'a necessary reassignment' in mind, and if he passed the initial assessment tests, in addition to the personal interview, he would be guaranteed a forty-five percent increase in his gross pay.

Myles, not one to argue with fate, passed the initial and then secondary assessment with flying colors. But then again, he always did. And when the interview came, he assumed it would be a breeze as well. But a few minutes into the conversation, he found himself sadly mistaken.

Myles stared at the woman opposite him on the screen and tried to reconcile the thoughts he had about her. On one hand, he found her insanely attractive—on the other, incredibly intense. In an uncomfortable sort of way. He both liked her and disliked her at the same time, and he wondered how this could be.

After grilling him for the better part of an hour via Skype, Myles was certain he was about to be turned down when Addison Hartman surprised him by offering him the job.

This was an important assignment, she'd insisted. He had better not mess it up, she'd warned. Something in her voice didn't sit right with Myles, and he immediately felt there was something personal about this assignment. Which wasn't altogether bad because Myles, true to form, had decided that should he ever come into contact with Mrs. Hartman, he wouldn't mind setting her straight, giving her something to be a little less intense about.

Aside from the above details, all he knew was that the client needed help getting 'back on her feet.' She needed someone who would push her without backing down and her agent felt that someone with his disposition would serve her client well. 'It must have to do with your time in the Navy,' she'd remarked, 'because I can clearly see that you're an Alpha—someone who isn't afraid to take charge… and to say that is exactly what this situation calls for would be a vast understatement,' she'd said.

No matter how many times he assured her he was up for the task she continued quizzing him repeatedly—this way and that way, on whether or not he understood what it was she was asking. And while Myles thought he understood, honestly, all he could think about at the moment was what it would be like to get away from the shithole of a town he'd been stuck in and to get down to Austin—where he'd find exactly what it was *he* needed. Women.

The selection around there had been limited to what amounted to a few 'regulars.' And if there was one thing Myles wanted less than anything these days, it was any sort of regularity. Especially concerning who was in his bed.

With that thought, he once again assured Mrs. Hartman that he could more than handle the job. In turn, she immediately sent him a plane ticket headed for Austin, which he then traded in for a bus ticket. Not so much because he needed the money, but because he considered flying indulgent given the bus was an option. And more importantly, because it had been too long and there was a stop he needed to make in a tiny North Texas town.

AS THE BUS PULLED INTO THE STATION, THE NEW FRIEND Myles had made on the bus nudged his shoulder with two fingers. Once, and then again, harder the second time.

"We're here!" the shrill voice announced in a way that instantly grated on his nerves.

Myles opened his eyes slowly so as to give the full effect. He hadn't really been sleeping. He'd only been pretending, which he found served as a helpful tactic to avoid a woman, which one had just picked up and slept with, yet remained stuck in close confinement with for the next several hours.

This one hadn't been too bad, he considered. She was pretty, but she talked too much. And she was young. At twenty, she was younger than he would have liked under normal circumstances. He did have standards, after all. Myles knew the girl's age just as he knew all his lover's ages. He'd applied the 'always determine their age first rule.' If finding out whether you were picking up jailbait were a game, and it was, these were the rules:

First, he stated his age. Then he offered to guess the females age by offering up a smaller number than he reasonably presumed—smaller by at least a half decade until she threw out a number stating her actual age.

Second, he in turn took considerable time (one had to be patient) insisting that no way did she look anywhere near *that* age. He assured them that they had to be pulling his leg— that they looked at minimum two to three years younger than they'd just stated.

Finally, they ended up pulling out their ID just to prove him wrong, and to no doubt, reinforce the point they subconsciously felt he was trying to make and that they would age well and thus, were acceptable long-term mates.

Once the real number was on the table, he always managed to feign shock. It was in his favor to let them win. Worked like a charm every time. Side note, the older the woman, the less the need for proof in the form of identification, but nonetheless, the age tactic still tipped the odds in favor greatly that he would get laid, and he was always more than generous in his subtraction.

Anyhow, *twenty* it was today, despite his slight reservation. At thirty-five, twenty just seemed *so* young. But Myles couldn't really help himself. He'd been desperate for variety over the past few months. So, when she'd smiled at him with that hopeful, naive look upon her face and batted her eyes in a terrible attempt at playing coy, Myles knew he wouldn't have to work too hard for this one. And he didn't. He spent fifteen minutes listening to her life story, combined with future aspirations. There was five more minutes' worth of stories told about the time he spent in the military—all of which were true, of course—despite his hearty appetite for one night stands, one thing Myles didn't believe in was lying.

Twenty minutes in—and he had her up against the bathroom door. A mere fifteen minutes after that, she had positioned herself so close to him that she was partway in his seat and was yapping in his ear as he pretended to doze off into oblivion. When he felt the pull of the bus slowing and coming to a stop, he felt himself literally exhale in relief.

As soon as the bus came to a complete stop, and not a second later, Myles stood, grabbed his duffle bag and carefully made sure to avoid eye contact.

She stood abruptly. *This was going to be more difficult than he'd hoped. It somehow always was.* "Hey. Give me your phone and I'll put my number in it," her shrill voice demanded.

Myles stared at the line that had quickly formed in the aisle and wished he'd chosen a seat closer to the front. "I don't have a phone."

"Oh, come on, I'm not falling for that!"

"Okay, then don't."

"You know, I really like you," she said as she fished around in her oversized bag. She pulled a card out and pushed it in his direction. "Here's my number. Call me."

Myles met her gaze then. *Best to be direct, he thought.* "I don't think so."

She scoffed. "Are you kidding me?"

Myles averted his gaze toward the front of the bus and wondered what the holdup was. He needed to get off this bus. *Fast.* "No."

The girl turned in every direction and looked at the passengers around them. Myles presumed that this was in hopes that one of them might come to her defense. She shook her head slightly. "I don't understand."

Finally, the line began to move. He ushered her out into the aisle and placed his hand at the small of her back. This served two purposes. One, it proved he could be a gentleman despite what alarms were likely going off in her head. And two, the gesture calmed her by putting him in control. He understood that her type needed this more than others might.

"So, you're serious? You're really not going to call?" She turned and asked as they approached the door.

Myles could smell the fresh air and practically taste freedom. He pressed his hand in a little harder to remind her to keep moving. "That's correct."

As the girl stepped off the bus, she turned and watched as he did the same. She let her bag sink to the ground dramatically. "Well, why not?" She then began to cry. People were beginning to stare.

Myles acted quickly. He stepped forward and kissed her cheek. He pulled back, looked her in the eye before leaning in and placing his mouth against her ear. "Because you're a beautiful, smart girl, and much too good for someone like me."

She pulled back forcefully, wiped her eyes, and placed her hands on her hips. "That's a bullshit excuse and you're an asshole!" she shouted.

But Myles had already turned to go.

For the briefest of moments, he considered that perhaps his delivery could've been a little more subtle.

Myles knew he was never going to call, so he figured why lie?

He was many things, he thought to himself, but a liar wasn't one of them.

MYLES ENTERED THE DARK, SMOKE-FILLED BAR TO FIND THAT not much had changed. From the music to the patrons to ol' Sammy the bartender, it was in many ways as though he'd never left at all.

"Well, well, would ya look what the cat dragged in?" Sammy called out to everyone and no one before hastily slapping a whiskey sour on the bar. Myles dropped his bag at his feet and perched himself on the bar stool. He extended his hand, but Sammy one-upped him and reached in for a hug, slapping him on the back so hard he nearly choked. "It's good to see you back here, man. Looks like the service has been treatin' you well."

Myles leaned back on the barstool. "Actually, I'm out."

The man appeared confused. "You're out. Ha! Nah, not you. You're a lifer." He waved his hand in the air to dismiss Myles. "Everyone around here always knew that about you, Ingram…with your big fancy medals and your name in the papers…"

Myles winced. It occurred to him that sometimes people weren't ready for the truth and this time counted as one of them. "Well, nonetheless, I'm headed to Austin. On a different kind of assignment."

The man laughed. "Top secret, eh? Well, hell, whaddaya say we get ya all liquored up and see how quick you forget it was ever a secret?"

Myles eyed the drink in front of him. *An evil he'd long ago learned to say no to.* "Thanks, Sam, but I think I'll just have water if you don't mind."

The bartender reached for a glass, dumped a few ice cubes in, filled it with the spigot, and placed it in front of him. "You all right, boy? I reckon I know why you came in here, and I'm sorry, son, but I gotta tell ya, the answer's still the same."

Myles raised his brow in understanding. He certainly wasn't surprised by the news he'd just been given, but knowing didn't stop the sting. He downed the glass of water, placed it back on the bar, and let out a long sigh. "Life is good, Sammy. No complaints here."

"I'm sorry, Lieutenant. I know this ain't what you wanted to hear. That's why you came in here and all…"

Captain, you mean. It was Captain now. Myles thought, but he didn't correct the man. Instead, he handed him a card. "No worries, my friend. Hey… listen. This is the number where I'll be staying. If you hear anything, *anything* at all, give me a call. Okay?"

The old bartender stared at the card as he flipped it over in his hands. He didn't look Myles in the eye when he answered, but then again, he didn't have to. "I sure will."

Myles nodded. *Old habits die hard, he thought.*

He didn't argue. He knew better this time. He simply stood, picked up his bag, and slapped a twenty on the bar. He nodded one last time at ol' Sammy, and then he turned and didn't look back.

CHAPTER SIX

Myles had been on the job for approximately three days before he met his boss. Instead, upon his arrival, a man, who introduced himself as Dean, the Clemens Family's butler, greeted him at the front gate. Dean was an ogre of a man and about what one might expect from a butler. Round, bald, and well, slightly past his prime. Myles didn't immediately like or dislike the man, but nonetheless, he got the sense that the both of them wondered why the other was there. The butler ushered him onto a golf cart and told Myles they were headed for his living quarters, which were to be separate from the rest of the staff's residence. There simply wasn't room for him, Dean informed him with a hint of a smile.

They passed an expansive colonial style house, a pool, and tennis courts, rounded a bend and stopped in front of one of the nicest barns Myles had ever seen. Dean parked the golf cart, killed the ignition, and then ushered Myles around to the side of the barn and up a flight of stairs. He pulled a massive key ring from his suit pocket, which contained a dozen or more keys attached to it and used one of them to unlock the door. Myles watched as he deftly removed the key from the ring and handed it to him. Dean turned the knob and ushered him inside the small but homey space. The place reminded Myles of a country cottage he'd perhaps once seen in a magazine, the kind that looked expensive and rarely lived in. He scanned the room, noting the bed and a desk where a Mac computer sat. There was also a small sofa and a restroom that he ducked his head into and found that while small, it still contained both a shower and a tub.

"You'll have to come down to the staff quarters for meals. We have a kitchen and a dining room there," the man said.

Myles nodded. "This is a nice space."

The butler looked at the ground and then up again staring out the window. "It used to be the Missus's writing room." He sighed. "Although, lucky for you I guess, she hasn't done much of that in quite some time now...." He paused and exhaled before continuing. "But given her injury, the stairs do admittedly pose a bit of a problem."

Myles shifted his stance and set down his duffle bag.

Dean abruptly turned toward the door. "Well, you have the key so I'll leave it to you to get settled."

Myles cleared his throat. *He wanted to tell the man not to worry, he wouldn't be taking his job—that he was an in and out sort of guy, but he sensed that he wouldn't have listened anyway. It bothered him that the guy seemed to have known something he didn't.* But he didn't say any of it. Instead, he simply posed a more clear-cut question. "Am I to report to you when I'm finished?"

If Myles wasn't mistaken, he thought he saw the man flinch. Slowly, Dean turned around and pulled a two-way radio and a folded note from his pocket. "Oh, right. I almost forgot." He handed the items to Myles and then ran his hand over his shiny bald head before continuing. "This here is a list of things which need attending to around the property as well as a map." He eyed Myles up and down. "I reckon it should keep you busy for a while. The radio… is how the staff communicates. Keep it with you and turned on at all times. Also, and this is important, you don't have access to the main house, so make sure to stay clear until you're told otherwise."

Myles twisted the knob on the radio, which brought it to life and with it a million memories came flooding back.

He shook his head slightly, needing to gain his bearings, although not enough for the man to take notice. Distracted, he unfolded the paper and stared at the list even though his mind was far from the words on the page. "Looks like I'd better get to it then."

The butler turned toward the door once again, and without saying a word, shut it a little harder than necessary behind him.

MYLES PUT THE FEW BELONGINGS HE OWNED AWAY AND THEN unfolded the map and studied it. He read the list and laid out a plan in his mind. Twenty-seven minutes later, he was onto the first task—to fix a portion of the wooden fence that lined the property. He gathered the tools he would need from the barn, located a half empty toolbox covered in dust, and went to work. It was warm that day, especially so early in the spring season, even for Texas. But Myles didn't mind the heat. Or the labor-intensive work. He found it meditative in the sense that it took his mind off things and kept him focused. It was just him and the sun and a fence that needed mending. He stayed out until dusk, finding that the fence needed a little more work than the list had suggested. He sat for a moment in the grass admiring his handiwork and watched the sun sink lower in the sky before heading back.

He was sweaty and tired, and for this, he was grateful because it was a good indication that this might actually be a good night—one in which sleep did not elude him, as it so often did these days.

As Myles entered the barn to return the tools, he rounded the corner and stopped dead in his tracks. He watched the brown haired woman, who was standing with her back to him as he quietly placed the toolbox at his feet.

He stood back up steadily and started toward her, one foot in front of the other. Halfway there, he stopped, lowered his voice and spoke slowly. "I could be mistaken but... I'm not sure you've fully thought this through..."

The woman flinched upon hearing his voice and he could tell he'd startled her—that she hadn't known he was there. As she spun to face him, she eyed him up and down. Myles didn't takes his eyes from her gaze noticing that the color of her eyes were a shade of green that he was pretty sure he'd never seen before.

"What I mean is... the knot you have there isn't going to do the trick."

"Excuse me?" she said with considerable contempt.

"Well, it's just that the rope isn't tied in a way that will bear your weight, that's all."

She cocked her head to the side. "Are you saying I'm fat?"

Myles noticed how her words slurred as she spoke. *She wasn't fat. Not even close. She was tiny and clearly, any person who offered that argument up couldn't be reasonably sane, which made sense given the circumstances.* "No. But wouldn't you say that's a bit irrelevant at this point."

"I don't care if you're calling me fat," she scoffed.

He took a step forward, instantly knowing it was a bad idea.

She pulled the rope tighter around her neck. "Stay back or I'll let go," she said almost breathlessly.

Myles put his hands up to show he understood and to assure her that he wasn't moving. "Here, I'll even sit down and enjoy the show. How's that?"

"Are you mocking me?" she said, sweeping the almond colored hair from her face.

"No. I just want to stick around and see how you're gonna get yourself out of this one." He grinned and then continued. "You've gotten yourself in quite the predicament here. It's gonna be tough to get down from there... the way you have yourself positioned and all."

The woman cocked her head and squinted, clearly sizing him up once again. "Yeah, well, I'll be dead so it appears that it'll be your problem, doesn't it."

"Nah."

She followed his eyes down and noticed that he was staring at the briefest hints of her midriff peeking through, huffed, and quickly adjusted her t-shirt. In doing so, she stumbled a little but managed to regain her balance.

Myles flinched and took a deep breath trying to steady himself.

"You won't do it. I know it. And you know it."

She laughed, and it was so unexpected, it concerned him more than he cared to admit. *Every warning bell inside his head was blaring. This woman is crazy. Not simply drunk, but certifiable.* She pointed directly at him and spoke matter of factly. "The fact that the color of your face is the same as that white t-shirt you're wearing begs to differ."

He shook his head. "If you were going to jump, you would've already done it—"

She straightened her stance before cutting him off. "Well, I would have if you hadn't so rudely interrupted me."

"What I was going to add was that it wouldn't matter anyhow. That knot wouldn't hold, the rope would break, and you'd simply fall on your ass. Best-case scenario, you'd break your legs—worst case, your legs and back. No worries, though. You'd still be alive to enjoy all that fun. And you'd probably hate yourself more and more every day... the least of those reasons being your inability to properly tie a knot."

"You're an asshole, you know that?"

He flashed his winning smile. "So I've been told. But the real name's Myles. And I assume you must be Jessica."

She seemed surprised. "How do I know what you're saying is true anyway?"

"That's easy. I never lie."

She frowned. "That's impossible. Everyone lies."

Myles dusted his palms against his pants. *"I'm* not everyone."

She smirked ever so slightly at this. *It was a good sign, Myles knew.* "Okay, Mr. *'not everyone.'* So what am I supposed to do now?"

"In other words, you're asking me how you get the job done?"

"Yes. That's exactly what I'm asking."

"Well, with all due respect, you do seem to be pretty liquored up. Couldn't you just wait a little while and let alcohol poisoning work it's magic?"

"Fuck you."

"It's a much more pleasurable way to off yourself is all I'm saying." He stood. "Look, this conversation has been fun, but if you don't mind, I have work to do. So, the way I see it, you have two options. One, you let me help you down. Or two, you stay up there and continue to weigh your options."

"I could fire you and solve that problem for you."

"You're the boss, I guess. But you could kill yourself getting down too, saving us both the trouble. I guess we could consider that a viable option three."

She huffed dramatically and lifted the rope from around her neck. She let it go, placed her hand on her hip, and then nodded at the bottle of liquor at her feet. "Option four, you hand me the bottle and I'll let you help me down."

He eyed the bottle and let out a hard sigh. "I hand you that bottle and you're getting down yourself."

"Fine."

Myles did as he'd agreed and placed the bottle in her hands. Then he put the tools back in their place, fled up the stairs, and took a long cold shower.

An hour later he went back down to the barn and found his new boss sitting on the table he'd left her standing on. She took a slow swig as she watched him come toward her. The table was fairly high, even at six-foot-two, he had to hop in order to perch himself beside her. He stared straight ahead as he spoke. "Trouble getting down, huh."

She placed the bottle between her legs. "Something like that."

A long pause had hung in the air before she spoke again. "I'm not crazy, you know."

"That's not for me to determine…"

"My husband left me."

"It happens."

"Not to me it doesn't."

He looked at her then. *She was rather beautiful, he thought. Though definitely not his type.* "The fact that you're stuck on top of a table, drunk, *and* trying to kill yourself begs to differ with that sentiment."

She turned toward him then and smiled a little. "Addison sent you didn't she?"

"If Addison is Mrs. Hartman, then yes."

"Myles, did you say it was?" she asked a puzzled look upon her face.

"Last time I checked."

"I think I need your help getting down."

Myles didn't respond, he simply hopped up and scooped

her into his arms. With few words between them, he managed to find her bedroom, place her in bed, and tuck her in. *Sleep it off, he thought. You'll feel better in the morning.* Myles broke the first two of many rules that night. One, he entered the main house, and two, he found he actually gave a damn. It also wouldn't hurt to mention—that night, he slept like a baby.

CHAPTER SEVEN

J ess ran the wet washcloth over her face once more and peered at her reflection in the mirror. *Not too bad, she thought. Considering.* She reached for one of the orange bottles on her bathroom counter, picked it up, and studied the contents. She'd need a refill soon. *Hadn't she just had this one filled?* It was hard to say she finally decided. Each day as of late seemed not all too different from the one previous. *Maybe she should do a better job at tracking her usage... she considered.*

Jess popped two pills in her mouth and swallowed. She placed a glass underneath the tap, filled it, and quickly rinsed the bitter aftertaste away. *Better.* It wouldn't be long and she'd feel better. She checked her reflection once more. *Today is a new day.* Today was going to be the first day of her new life, she decided. Since she'd attempted suicide and survived, she assured herself what better time than now, than today, to make a fresh start. *Yes, a plan! Why hadn't she seen this sooner?* A plan was exactly what she needed. Jess considered this for a moment and promptly began frantically searching her bathroom and then her bedroom for a pen. She turned everything inside out and upside down looking. *How hard was it to find a bloody pen in this place?*

Upon hearing the commotion, one of the maids peeked in, her hand instinctively flew to her chest as she surveyed the contents of the room turned astray.

"May I help you with something madam?" the girl asked gently.

Jess straightened herself and eyed the mess she'd just created. "Yes. I would really like a pen. And a notepad." She inhaled deeply. "Oh... and what time is it? Have the children left for school yet?"

"No, ma'am. They're down for breakfast. It's just seven o'clock."

"Wonderful, then let them know I'll be driving them today."

The maid met Jessica's gaze just briefly then nodded before lowering her gaze back down to the floor and closing the door behind her.

This was wonderful! The day was already shaping up well. Jess didn't need a pen or a notepad, she decided. The plan had already begun taking shape in her mind. First, she would drive the kids to school, and then she would attend her first yoga class since... well, *since...* before.

It was time. She would get back to her regular routine, get herself in shape again, and then surely, Spencer would come back. She silently chided herself for not seeing things so clearly all along. It had been a week and a half since Spencer had walked out of their bedroom and seemingly, right out of her life. And Jess found that she missed him more than she considered she might that afternoon as she watched him pack his bags. *She should've fought harder. He would've stayed, if only she'd asked.*

Instead, he was headed to Africa for a month (maybe two) on a safari, something he said he'd always wanted to do, or so he had written anyway in an email sent the evening he left. He'd written her exactly three emails since that time, mostly all business, and what wasn't business simply said to hug the children for him and give them his love. Neither Jonathan nor Catherine had said much about their father or his absence. It really wasn't anything out of the ordinary to them. Spencer had never really been a regular staple in his kid's day-to-day lives. His typical work day consisted of him coming home well after their bedtime and sometimes, he left before Jess woke them for school. But this had been during the 'old days' before the accident. After the accident, he hung around the estate more often, usually seeing that Jess's needs were attended to and that all was running as it should. That's not to say that he was necessarily around all that much either, the way Jess remembered it. Their property was a fairly large one and her husband had always been somewhat good at making himself scarce when he wanted to. In the beginning of their marriage, this bothered her more than it did after the children came along, once her days were filled with catering to their needs or seeing that someone did. It was just how things were as her mother had assured her time and time again. Men in their family tended to the family business, which really just meant 'managed their wealth and investments' while the women made their lives easy. In turn, this allowed them to do what they did best.

But Jess and her mother had differing opinions on what their men did best. The way Jess saw it, Spencer was best at smoking cigars, drinking the approximate amount of scotch so as not to overdo oneself all the while rubbing elbows with his elitist friends, friends of his elitist friends, and so forth. This isn't to say that their marriage was unhappy— it wasn't.

They played couples tennis on Tuesdays, Thursdays, and Saturdays. They went to dinner with the Evans every other Friday. They had regular sex. Even if it was scheduled. Who wasn't scheduling these days? Her mother had remarked when Jess once wondered aloud whether or not doing so was 'normal.' The two of them took regular vacations and though Jessica often fretted about the state of their relationship, there was nothing she could directly pinpoint that seemed amiss. Marriage served its purpose (according to her mother) and Jess always made sure to fill her time with interests of her own, which in turn, seemed to make her husband happy. *He just needed a break, she decided, standing there in her bathrobe.*

And today was a new day and this 'break' was an opportunity— at a new life, one in which her husband wouldn't need to take a sabbatical from.

Jessica eyed the bottle of vodka at her bedside table and considered having a drink. Then she thought back on the previous night and where the drinking had gotten her. To Jessica's frustration, she realized that it would've been nice if she had figured this new way of living out last night, prior to meeting the newest member of her staff. *What in the hell was Addison thinking sending him anyway?* Jess made a mental note to add calling her best friend to the growing list of things she would accomplish today. The way that man had looked at her, with such irreverence, had rattled her. She still felt uneasy about it this morning. She then added 'do something about the new staff member' to her ever-growing list. But first things first. She marched into her massive closet and grabbed the perfect workout outfit to make herself presentable.

Jess was getting around these days pretty well. She still had a fair amount of pain and walked with a slight limp, which occasionally caused her to have to use a cane, depending on what kind of day it was. If she'd experienced a moderate amount of pain and needed to take more than the recommended dose of pain pills at her disposal then she would surely need to use the cane, if for no other reason than to steady herself and make it appear as though she were less high than in actuality. On the other hand, if it was a good day, such as today, Jess could manage on her own with a little help from the narcotics, which were all lined up on her bathroom counter. In addition to the pills, a nurse regularly made house calls to give her injections, and if it had been a particularly rough week, she'd receive a complimentary fentanyl patch. These were nice, this way she didn't have to try to keep track of how many pills she was actually taking.

Jess dressed in her favorite Lulu Lemon yoga pants and tank top and pulled her hair up into a bun. She then added a touch of powder, mascara, and lipgloss to seal the deal. She eyed the bottle again before deciding against it and turning to study herself in the mirror. *Not too bad. Considering.* She stood a little taller, checked her appearance one last time in the mirror, and mostly satisfied, smiled at her reflection. 'Operation: win her husband back' had just officially commenced.

JESS CHECKED THE TIME ON HER PHONE AS SHE PRESSED THE elevator button. She frowned, no time for breakfast. *That's okay. She wasn't really hungry anyway.* They'd need to leave soon or the kids would be tardy. Finally, the door opened and Jess stepped inside. She pressed the down button and leaned her forehead against the cool glass mirror. Her head was now throbbing no doubt in response to the sheer volume of alcohol she'd consumed the night before. She fumbled around in her bag until she felt the smooth vial touch her fingertips. She pulled it out, counted the pills, and shook it for good measure, thinking one more couldn't hurt. *Just enough to take the edge off.*

The elevator doors opened, and all of a sudden, real life hit her hard. Her senses were overloaded with the house suddenly coming to life. From the sound of her children arguing to dishes being washed and put away, noise filled the air. It was almost too much. She needed to get out of there. Jess rushed in to find Jonathan and Catherine sitting at the bar. "Hurry. Grab your things, we're going to be late."

Catherine clapped her hands instantly. "Wait. Mommy, you're driving us today?"

Jess nodded. "I sure am. And then I'm going to yoga."

"Yay!

"Shh." She kissed the top of her daughter's head. "Make sure to tell Daddy all about it the next time he calls, okay?"

Jonathan shook his head, eyed her up and down, and then headed for the door.

Jessica watched him go when suddenly, Dean, the family butler appeared at the bar, followed by the maid who she'd asked to retrieve a pen. *Jess couldn't for the life of her remember the woman's name.* Dean spoke in a serious tone. "Mrs. Clemens, I'm not sure this is a good idea, you driving the children."

"I'm not sure I asked for your opinion, Dean," Jess replied sharply.

"Yes, I understand. It's just that you haven't been given clearance from the doctor to drive."

She stood and waved him off. "I most certainly have. And, Dean... Watch it. These are *my* children. I believe I know what's best for them."

The butler pursed his lips and simply nodded as Jess

reached for her daughter's hand, smiled, and together, they bounced out the door.

JESS COULDN'T RECALL WHAT SHE AND THE CHILDREN CHATTED about that morning on the way to school. She only remembered the relief she felt at being 'back in the game.' She did, however, remember running late and pulling into the parking spot clearly marked 'McCain Family Parking' which her former friend and Ladies Who Lunch President had heftily paid for in the school auction. She'd surely already come and gone, Jess decided upon seeing it empty.

It wasn't like Shannon to be late for anything, ever. In addition, this year, according to her 'new life plan,' she would make sure to outbid the McCain's for that spot by at least ten fold. In her old life, Jess had thought such a thing as bidding over a parking spot was ridiculous. But today was a new day and such a thing no longer seemed silly anymore, especially on the off chance that one were running late. Plus, Jess gathered, this was the sort of thing her husband would enjoy, him being the flashier of the two. Luxuries like this, for Spencer, always were about principle and status, and Jess considered for once that maybe her husband's philosophy on 'eat or be eaten' might be somewhat accurate.

She would tell him as much, she noted mentally, as she put the car in park and eyed her children in the rearview mirror.

"You're coming in?" her son asked, rolling his eyes.

Catherine waited expectantly for her answer.

Jess looked back and forth between the two of them before stopping on her son. "I tell you what. If you tuck in your shirt, I'll let you get a one-minute head start. I'll walk your sister in… since *she's* not yet *too* cool to be seen with me."

She winked at her daughter. "Boys."

"I don't like tucking in my shirt."

Jess huffed. "Your father and I pay a lot of money for you to attend this school and that's the rule here, so the least you can do is respect it… and our contribution to your future."

Jonathan unbuckled his seatbelt. "But *why* is it a rule? Does anyone really know? I think it's something that someone a long time ago made up and we all just follow blindly. Plus, you're not exactly one to talk. I'm pretty sure that last name on the sign above this parking space *isn't* ours…"

Jess considered this for a moment. *He had a point.* "If you want to challenge the rules, go ahead, son. But you need to be prepared with an argument a little bit more valid than other people bend the rules so I am going to, too. So long as you understand this—you can wear your shirt upside down and inside out for all I care."

Her son shot her a look that only confirmed she'd missed the mark on so many levels. He raised his brow, climbed out, and slammed the door.

Jessica sighed. *She needed to do something about him. His anger concerned her.* She added this to her mental list, ushered Catherine out of the backseat, and grabbed her backpack. No sooner had she turned to close the car door, had she heard the honking horn. She turned slowly to see none other than Shannon McCain pulled up aside her, window rolled down. *Great. So she was occasionally late.* Jessica flashed her best shit-eating grin.

Shannon eyed her daughter up and down. "Hello, Catherine," she said in a voice an octave too high before turning her attention to Jessica and lowering it by at least a dozen. "It's good to see you're feeling better and that you are out and about. But certainly, you're aware you're parked in my spot."

Jess cocked her head to the side, glanced back at the 'McCain Family Parking' clearly noted on the sign, and then turned back toward her former friend. "Oh, yes, about that," she lied, "I'm surprised that no one notified you... It seems that the school doesn't have adequate handicap parking. I took the issue up with administration and until we can all come up with a better solution... it seems I'll need to utilize this spot. It's really a good thing I realized this before someone at the city did and had fined the school. They were pretty thankful. Those fines can be quite hefty I hear. "

Shannon's eyes grew wide and her face reddened. She frowned, exhaled rather loudly, raised her window, and sped off without so much as another glance in Jess's direction.

Jess smiled at her daughter. She really should have considered using the disabled angle before. It would certainly save her the time, effort, and money trying to outbid Shannon McCain. *Her husband would be proud, she thought.* She'd make sure to tell him all about it the next time they spoke.

THE YOGA STUDIO WAS CROWDED BY THE TIME JESS ARRIVED. She checked in at the front desk and proceeded into her usual spot only to find that it was taken. She quickly picked a new one, rolled out her mat, and carefully made her way down to the floor—a feat that proved more difficult than she had neither hoped for nor expected.

Jess focused on her reflection in the mirror, tried to make herself appear taller, and did her best to avoid small talk. She noticed a few sideways glances and there were a few brave women who approached her to say that they were glad to see her back, but for the most part, her fellow yogi's simply avoided her all together. To those that did approach, Jess was courteous but made it clear she wasn't really in the mood for small talk. Once she began stretching, she questioned whether or not she was really up for the hour-long hot yoga class. Sure, there would be several postures that she would need to avoid, if not most of them, now that she gave it some thought—the same way she needed to avoid many of the women in the room, but yoga was about mind-body connection and while her body may not work the way it once had, she settled on the fact that her mind was fine.

Jess settled in and reached for her toes. Instantly, she felt searing pain. *Perhaps this was a bad idea, she considered. Too much. Too soon.* But she wasn't leaving now that everyone had seen her arrive. *People talk.* She could do hard things, she silently assured herself. She *had* to do hard things if she wanted to get her life back on track.

To help get her through, she reached into her bag and grasped the pill bottle in her hand. With the other, she twisted the cap and calmly fished a pill out. She glanced around the room and noticed a few women quickly averted their gaze. *Calm down.* No one had seen the bottle, she noted. *They're just rudely curious about the gimp who thought it would be a good idea to show up for yoga.* Jess looked around the room once more, and satisfied that no one seemed to be paying her any mind, she quietly slipped the pill into her mouth and swallowed. *This would get her through. Just until she was stronger.*

This was the last thought Jessica remembered having prior to awakening sometime later on a gurney. She surveyed her familiar surroundings, sighed, and pulled herself upright to a seated position. Seated adjacent to her, immersed in a book, was Myles, her new employee. The one she hadn't gotten around to having Addison fire. Jess squeezed her temples and eyed the blonde haired, clean cut, oversized man. *He was huge. Proportionally huge.* He didn't look up so she broke the silence. "I take it yoga didn't go so well…"

He placed a bookmark between the pages and met her gaze head on in a way that made her instantly uncomfortable. His eyes were such a pale shade of blue that they practically cut right through her.

"I'd say that's an understatement."

CHAPTER EIGHT

hat a dumb fucking thing to do, Myles wanted to scream at her. But he refrained himself knowing all too well this wasn't likely to go over well. Instead, he took a more direct approach. "Are you trying to have your children taken away?"

Myles eyed Jessica, who picked at a thread on her hospital gown. It took all he had not to take his thumbs and gently wipe the mascara that had smeared beneath her eyelids. He wanted to reach for her chin and force her to look at him. He wanted to shake her. He wanted to ask her what in the hell she was thinking and to tell her how ignorant he thought she was for taking so much for granted. Mostly though, he wanted to know why he cared so much in the first place. "Answer me, Jessica."

She frowned and slowly met his eye. "What do you think?"

"Since you asked… I think driving under the influence is a really dumb fucking thing to do. Doing so, with your kids in the car… well, that's pretty hard to top."

She cocked her head to the side. "Why *are* you here, anyway?"

He wanted to tell her that her staff had picked him because no one else wanted to clean up her mess, but figured maybe it wasn't the best approach. "It's my job."

Jessica glared at him. "Well, I'm relieving you of that." She nodded at the door. "You're free to go."

Myles brushed his forehead as if to say *whew*. "Everything has always come so easy to you, hasn't it? If I had to guess... I'd say you're a daddy's girl, who never wanted for much..." *Did she have any idea how much he would give to be in her shoes? Just once more, even if for a day, just so he could get it right.*

She shot him a go to hell look, which told him everything he already knew. He sat back in his chair, crossed his arms behind his head, and leaned back against them. He stared at her for a second too long and then up at the ceiling. "I'm afraid it's not that simple. I'm under contract..."

Jessica changed the subject. "When is the doctor coming back? I need something for my head. And I need to get out of here."

"No. What you need is to give in to the pain. Stop relying on substances to fix your problem."

"Don't tell me what *I* need to do. Who in the fuck are you to talk to me about pain? *You* seem to get around just fine."

The doctor entered then. She glanced from Myles to Jessica and cleared her throat. She looked down at the chart she held in her hand, and then extended the opposite to shake Jessica's hand. The woman, all business, no fun, he'd accessed, eyed him as he sat up in his chair. "You must be Mr. Clemens?"

He shook his head. "No."

She appeared confused but continued. "Jessica, it appears that you pushed your limits a little too far this morning... after reviewing your recent medical history, I would advise against Hot Yoga for the foreseeable future. The CT scan came back clear, which confirms my suspicions that it was over-exertion that caused the fainting episode."

Myles watched Jessica as the doctor spoke. He noted the way her eyes lit up when she realized she hadn't been found out. *Give an inch, they take a mile*. "Can I have something for my head?" she asked. "I must have hit it when I went down…"

The doctor checked the chart again. "Absolutely. I'll call down to the pharmacy and order something up. In the meantime, we'll probably keep you here for another hour or so for observation. Just to make sure."

"Are you sure that's a good idea, doc? The medication, I mean. I wouldn't want to mask the symptoms if there were an underlying condition."

The woman gave a hard smile. *Clearly, no one questioned her authority either.* "That's a very valid concern. But I'm just prescribing a little something to take the edge off. Mrs. Clemens has been through a lot this morning. The stress of it is likely contributing to the headache."

Myles nodded. "I see."

He watched Jessica's face as his suggestion was shot down. When the doctor pulled the curtain, Jessica winked at him. She held his gaze. "I guess it really is just like you said… it's pretty amazing how everything comes so easily for me."

Myles watched her lips as she spoke and imagined giving her a little something to quiet that smart mouth of hers.

Instead, he shook his head and decided that suddenly, he too, needed something to take the edge off.

THERE'S A CERTAIN LOOK A PERSON HAS IN THEIR EYE THAT always tells him they also suffer from what ails him. It could

be loneliness, it could be pain—sometimes it was boredom...
but whatever it was, he learned to spot it a mile away.

Today it happened to be a nurse restocking hospital
rooms. As Myles walked the corridors under the guise of
searching for coffee, he noticed her immediately. He noticed
right away the way she met his eye and then looked at the
floor before looking back up at him again. *A sign of submission.* He passed her up and then turned back and asked for
directions to the cafeteria. A mere ten minutes and a small
chat later, he had her bent over a shelf in the supply closet,
his hand covering her mouth. When they'd both finished, he
watched her re-dress as he disposed of the condom in the
appropriate medical waste container. *He'd always had a thing
for nurses.* He straightened himself up and refastened his belt,
and then he leaned in and kissed her forehead, telling her
that they should meet again. Knowing they never would.

Myles didn't wait for her to respond. He turned the lock
and pushed the door open just slightly.

"You go first," he'd whispered ushering her out. "I'll wait
here for a minute."

The girl smiled. *This wasn't her first rodeo.*

Satisfied, albeit temporarily, he tucked in his shirt and
exited shortly behind her.

Once he was in the clear, he stopped and leaned against
the wall. He cleared his mind before making his way back
down to the emergency room. He may make risky choices,
but at least he was always safe. He had nothing left to lose
anyway. And he could stop anytime he wanted to.

This was more than he could say for that boss of his.

～

"WHAT THE HELL HAPPENED TO YOU?" SHE'D ASKED WHEN HE

returned, her tone giving everything away. *Women always knew. He figured they smelled it.*

Myles cocked his head to the side and looked her up and down. "I'd ask you the same thing, but I'm afraid I already know."

They both had their secrets—he was simply better at hiding his. But in her defense, she was smarter than he'd given her credit for. Don't get too close, he reminded himself. History always repeats itself.

She frowned. "You look like you just ran a marathon…"

He flashed the best shit-eating grin he could muster. "Maybe I did."

CHAPTER NINE

"**D**eclined?" She asked.

"Yes ma'am, I've tried it twice."

Jessica dug through her handbag and reached into her wallet. "Here, try this one."

The clerk gave her a look that was somewhere between sympathy and annoyance.

Jess touched the items she had placed on the counter and then looked back over at Myles, who was sitting in an over-sized chair rubbing at his temples. He'd been her permanent sidekick, much to both of their disappointment, ever since the Yoga incident. Jess couldn't help but notice how unhappy he looked, and wondered how long they would both be able to keep this up. She was a danger—not only to herself but to her children as well, a message her husband, mother, and best friend had so gently delivered a few days following her trip to the emergency room. Her husband by way of Skype. *Who hosts an intervention via Skype?* Jess had asked Myles at one point. She wasn't certain, but she was pretty sure he'd whispered, "Pussies, that's who," under his breath.

"I'm sorry, Mrs. Clemens. This one isn't working either.

We are able to hold your items for up to twenty-four hours…"

"She's holding up the line," a young twenty-something said aloud as though Jess herself wasn't aware of this fact and couldn't hear her. "But don't worry. She probably has another one to pull out, as if no one around here has *anywhere* to be," the girl continued. A few fellow shoppers murmured similar sentiments. Most just stared.

Jessica shifted her feet. Her leg was hurting pretty badly today as was her back. She needed to take something soon or else tomorrow would be worse. *The usual and agreed upon dosage wasn't doing it anymore.* "This is insane!" She found herself shouting a little louder than she'd intended. Additional shoppers were starting to take notice of her predicament no doubt, thanks to the snotty twenty-something and her huffing and puffing coming from the rear of the line. She took her credit card from the clerk's hand. "I need to make a phone call. I'll be back." Jess said as she turned, shoved her wallet back in her handbag, and glared at the loud-mouthed girl.

She'd intended to say something once she reached her, but as Jess made her way through the line, her leg gave out, and she fell. No one moved to help as Jessica tried in vain to pick herself up. The clerk came from around the counter and stared, her mouth open.

Immediately, Myles was at her side as she tried once again in vain to rise up off the floor. "Here, let me help," he whispered.

Jess intended to refuse his offer, she was embarrassed enough as it was, but when she met his gaze, she was surprised to see something in his eyes, something she hadn't seen before. She nodded before he grabbed just underneath her armpits with both hands and gently pulled her up. She steadied herself as Myles held her in place. "Are you dizzy?"

She shook her head. "My leg hurts."

Myles addressed the clerk. "Hold those items, the last name's Ingram." Then he turned, swiftly picked Jess up, and carried her out, parting the crowd in the process. If people hadn't been staring before, they certainly were now. But for the first time in a long time, Jessica Clemens found she didn't give a damn.

∾

THE LONG CAR RIDE HOME WAS MOSTLY A SILENT ONE UNTIL she interrupted the silence. "I don't understand why he would do this?"

Myles didn't respond right away and when he did, it wasn't what she expected. *It never was.* "It's none of my business, but I'm not sure how you didn't see this coming."

The fight had gone out of her. She was hurting too bad to put forth any real effort. "Well, I didn't."

Myles looked her way and studied her face. He started to speak and hesitated before starting again. "Do you want my opinion?"

Jess stared out the window. It was a cloudy day and a light rain had begun to fall, fitting weather for the occasion, she thought. "I don't know. Do I?"

"I guess I just have a hard time understanding how you let it happen."

She was disappointed with his response but not in the mood to fight. "Oh?"

Myles lowered his voice and focused his attention on the road. "I assume he has complete control of your finances."

Jess sighed. "Your assumption would be correct..."

"Sadly," was all he said in return.

"What am I going to do about it?"

He looked over then, offering a small smile. "I don't know… but I'm sure you'll figure something out."

Jess leaned her head against the cool glass window and closed her eyes.

There was nothing more she wanted to say and so she let the silence fill her up. *How could she have been so stupid to hand over not only all responsibility of her personal finances to her husband but also her family's fortune? She couldn't even recall exactly when this had happened or how the decision had been made. And to think she'd never once considered it a bad idea. She wasn't sure which was worse—the fact that she had done it to begin with or the fact that she hadn't known better.*

Myles interrupted her reverie. "Hey, Jess."

She opened one eye and peeked out in his direction.

"Try not to let that something be the pills, okay?"

Jess closed her eyes, curled up, and shifted to fully face the window. "Aye, aye, Captain."

Myles smiled to himself. *Captain.* It had been a long time since anyone had referred to him that way.

This wasn't so bad. Who knew what tomorrow would bring, but that day, they'd both gotten at least a few things right.

JESS WOKE THE FOLLOWING MORNING AND FOUND THAT THE pain was as bad as she'd expected. If not worse. She rolled over to grab the pills Myles had set out for her. Ever since the Yoga incident and subsequent intervention, her medication had been closely monitored. It was dished out to her at regular intervals and she was accompanied whenever she left the house. Of course, she hadn't agreed to these terms completely voluntarily. There was the threat of sending her back to rehab, or to a different rehab altogether, if she couldn't cope, a threat that weighed heavily on her mind.

She tossed the pills back and placed the glass of water back on her bedside table when something caught her eye. Hanging on a rack in her bedroom were none other than the pieces she'd picked out at Neiman Marcus the day prior. Jessica pulled herself to a seated position, then slowly stood, and made her way over to them. She grinned as she ran her hand over the fabric. There was a note attached to the top of one of the garment bags, which Jess removed and unfolded carefully.

These are on me. Get your shit together, though. I'm almost starting to like it here. —Myles

She carefully refolded the note and placed it in her nightstand drawer. She had an idea and quickly wondered how she'd missed this all along. It was all starting to make sense now.

Jess showered and dressed. She took two swigs off the bottle of vodka she had hidden in her closet drawer, instead of the usual three. She wasn't perfect, she had her secrets, but at least she knew her limits.

And, anyway, she had a plan.

JESS SAT IN HER NEW DRESS, SIPPING HER TEA AS SHE WATCHED the way Myles played with her daughter in the garden. She noticed the way her son had taken to him, and her son didn't take to very many.

"Nice dress." He nodded in her direction, slipping into one of the patio chairs opposite her.

"You're a natural, you know," she said catching him off guard.

He shrugged and looked away.

"You know, I was just thinking… I really don't know anything about you…"

"There's not much to know." He smiled, slipped out of the chair, and resumed playing keep-away from Catherine.

Jessica cleared her throat and shouted over the noise. "Catherine, it's time for your riding lesson."

"But I don't want to ride today!" her daughter yelled, placing her hands on her hips. "I want to stay and play with Myles."

She sighed. "Catherine—"

Myles interrupted by throwing Catherine over his shoulder. "Don't worry, I got this. I'll drive her down to the stable."

Jess shook her head. "Let Dean. I need to talk to you about something, actually."

He deadpanned. *Why did women have to make it so difficult?* "Well, there's only one problem… you see, I made a pinky promise. And I don't take pinky promises lightly."

Unable and unwilling to argue the value or relevance of a pinky promise, she watched them pull away, and then she picked up her cell and dialed Addison.

"I'm in trouble," Jess whispered when she answered.

Addison laughed. "You're telling me."

"No, I'm serious. Spence cut me off. He canceled my credit cards… I don't have access to our other accounts. "

Addison exhaled. "Oh. How very like Spencer."

"Yeah. Anyway, I have a plan. But I need your help… I'm going to send you an email outlining what I need here in a minute—"

Addison cut her off. "Jess, you need to call your attorney."

"Actually, I have a little something else in mind first." She eyed Myles coming around the bend in the Ranger. "But hey —I gotta go. Look for my email, will you?"

She clicked the phone off as Myles pulled up a chair and took a seat. He eyed her expectantly.

Jess smiled. "First off, thank you for picking up the clothes. You really didn't have to do that. And I realize that I don't exactly have cheap tastes so I'm having the agency reimburse you—"

"Wow." Myles sat up straighter and cut her off.

She looked confused. "What?"

"Nothing."

Myles changed his mind and leaned in close, propping his elbows on the table. "Can I ask you a question, Jessica?"

"Sure."

He smiled ruefully. "How many friends do you have?"

She didn't follow. "I don't know. Why?"

"I mean friends... that don't work for you. How many people are close to you who aren't on your payroll?"

She leaned back in her chair and crossed her arms. "That's a terrible thing to say."

"Then, I guess you know how it feels."

She still didn't follow. "How what feels?"

"Nothing. Anyhow, I'm not saying for sure or anything, but this *could* be a problem. The friend thing. You might want to take a look at your friend to employee ratio."

"You're an asshole. You know that?"

"I do. So, what was it you wanted to talk to me about? Other than my inability to keep up with your lifestyle."

"I didn't mean that—"

He leaned back and waited. She let it go.

"Do you have a passport?"

He nodded slowly.

Jessica grinned. "Good. Because we're going to Africa. To solve my husband-to-money problem."

Myles sighed. "Of course, we are."

~

A WEEK LATER, THE TWO OF THEM SAT SIDE BY SIDE IN FIRST class awaiting takeoff on the first leg of their journey to Kenya. Myles reached over, fastened her seat belt, and then his own. She eyed him suspiciously. "Did you just buckle me?"

He shrugged. "It's just what you do."

Jess cocked her head. "Have you ever traveled before?"

"A time or two."

She seemed surprised. "Where to?"

He stared over her shoulder and out the window. "Here and there."

She frowned and pulled the window shade shut. "You're such a great conversationalist. This trip is going to be thrilling, I can already tell."

He leaned over her and pushed it back up again. "It wasn't my idea."

She perked up at this sentiment. "Yeah, about that…, you know, I don't understand how I didn't see it all along! Sure, he had to force my hand, but I *finally* got it. It's so obvious that this is what he wanted. Me to chase him, I mean. Really, for me to fight for him. Spencer always did champion being a fighter. I just can't wait to see his face when he sees me! It's going to be so good."

Myles smiled. *And then she said that.*

~

CHAPTER TEN

J ess woke on the second leg of their flight to find the seat
next to her empty. She waited a few minutes for her
fellow traveler to return before deciding that a bathroom break wouldn't be a bad idea and that it would probably do her some good to stretch her legs and wash her face.
She found that the restrooms near first class were occupied
so she made her way to the rear of the plane only to discover
that the bathrooms there were in service as well. She leaned
on the door of one of them and waited before she gave up
and moved onto another set across the way where she was
hopeful she would have better luck. Jess silently prayed and
shifted from foot to foot realizing either she'd slept longer
than she'd thought or that she had vastly underestimated her
need to utilize the facilities.

She knocked once and waited. When there was no
response, she moved onto the next set and tried knocking
there. Still nothing. On the last set, she pounded a little
harder. After what felt like a tiny bit of eternity, she heard a
latch release and thanked the heavens when the door finally
opened. She breathed a sigh of relief, and made her way over

but realized her mistake and stepped back to allow for the occupant to step out. An attractive woman quickly brushed past her, but her eyes didn't meet Jessica's eyes. *Please don't let it smell.* Jess reached for the door only to feel it push back against her, catching her off guard. Myles stepped out leaving them both caught off guard. Instantly, his expression changed to one she couldn't quite read.

He exited the small space, held the door for her, and stepped aside. Jess glared and waited for him to say something, to give any explanation as to why he and that woman felt the need to share a restroom, but when nothing came, she closed the door behind her. Jessica stayed put in that bathroom longer than entirely necessary if for no other reason than so she didn't have to go back to her seat and face him. *What in the hell was he thinking? Did he even know that woman? And, worse, why did she even care?*

When Jess eventually did return to first class, Myles was asleep and she wasn't sure whether to be angry or relieved. Nonetheless, she took it upon herself to order a screwdriver and then another and another until the flight attendant politely refused her request for 'just one more.'

Jessica stared at Myles. *This was ridiculous.* She watched his oversized body as he slept. She watched the rise and fall of his massive chest as he breathed in and out. She noticed the way his large hands rested upon his flat stomach and wondered if she'd ever noticed any of these things before. She noted the way his bangs fell into his eyes and how she had to force herself not to brush them aside. Surely, she'd considered his appearance prior, but there was something about seeing him with that woman that made her feel *different. Protective.* The thought of his face as he'd exited that bathroom infuriated her. Jess huffed and puffed and shifted this way and that way in her seat hoping to wake him. Possibly simply because she was agitated, but more so because she was drunk and didn't care. Finally, unable to take it any longer she poked his shoulder hard. He shot straight up and eyed her suspiciously. "What the hell?" He looked around clearly startled.

"The plane is going down."

He stared blankly, looked around the cabin and apparently satisfied with what he saw, settled back into his seat. "Not funny."

"Listen, I need you to order a vodka and OJ. They won't let me have another. But if it's for you…"

"I don't drink."

She raised her voice louder. "Damn it, Myles. You know what I mean… don't fuck with me." She crossed her arms over her chest. "I'm not in the mood."

He studied her, then allowed his displeasure to play across his face. "Good grief, how many have you already had?"

"How many have *you* had?" She slurred her words.

He placed his hand on her forearm. *A warning.*

She sat up straighter and glared at him. "Well, how many?"

"Jessica, stop. Now."

"You stop. Who are you to tell me anything?" she hissed.

Myles shifted and faced her. He took her chin between his hands forcefully and stared directly into her eyes. "Listen to me. If you don't stop this right now, I will drop your ass the moment we get off this plane. Do you understand me? And I'm guessing, of all the foreign countries, this isn't one a woman like you wants to be dropped in, alone."

Jessica understood his limits, even if she wasn't willing to verbalize it. She pulled back and rubbed her chin. "That hurt."

Myles frowned. "Come here." He pulled her in his direction so that her head rested on his shoulder. She didn't move to pull away as they'd both expected. "Do not say another word," he whispered harshly. "Sleep it off."

They sat there quietly like that for some time, stiff—but unwilling to move. And then he felt her silent tears fall though she tried her best to conceal them.

"I know you're scared." He shushed her quietly. And though he couldn't pinpoint exactly why he'd said it, he added. "We all are."

THE TWO OF THEM FLEW INTO NAIROBI, THE CAPITAL AND largest city in Kenya, where a car met them at the airport and drove them to their hotel nearby. Once checked in, they went their separate ways. Myles freshened up in his room as Jessica sobered up in hers. In an hour, their driver was scheduled to arrive and take them to the camp where Jessica's husband was staying.

Myles showered and scrubbed the woman's scent off him. *He hadn't even liked this one.* It was rough and was exactly what he'd needed, but it had left him unsatisfied still, and to make matters worse, his boss had busted him. He checked his phone. Finally, he'd been given a lead that just might pan out when he was called away to Africa to deal with someone else's problems. *No new news.* Frustrated, he dressed and made his way to Jess's room. He was ready to let her have it, but when she opened the door, she appeared to be in better spirits. Not to mention the fact that she made him lose all train of thought. Myles had seen many women in his time, but Jessica Clemens was in another league. She was naturally beautiful. It wasn't so much in the way that she dressed, though that was a nice touch, or the way she expensively adorned herself, but it was simply her presence. The way she carried herself. Not his usual type, if there were such a thing these days. She was a category all her own. Regal, yet broken. She was the kind of woman who made a man feel like a man.

He cleared his throat and hoped his head would follow. *He knew thinking like this was dangerous territory. He was playing with fire.* "So what's the plan?"

She eyed his reflection in the mirror as she fastened her diamond earring. It had to be the biggest he'd ever seen. In person, anyway. "Plan? I'm here to get my husband back."

Myles looked away. "And your plan to do this is *what* exactly?"

"Spencer would never expect me to come all the way to Africa. You know, I said it before, but my gut tells me this really is what he wanted all along." She checked herself once more in the mirror, this time from the back, and grinned, apparently satisfied with her appearance. "Also, I mean… look at me."

He deadpanned and met her eye even though he knew she hadn't meant it literally. "I am."

She smiled playfully, but upon likely seeing the intensity he held within his gaze, he quickly watched her smile fade and give way to confusion.

He stood and walked to her. She stiffened, clearly unsure what his next move would be. Myles surprised her by reaching for her zipper. She gasped and then held her breath as he yanked it up the few inches she'd missed, or more likely, couldn't reach. His hand brushed the back of her neck as he caught the end and her eyes met his. He spoke slowly not taking his eyes off hers. "I just think you should be prepared, that's all. You should know what you're going to say… know what you came here for."

She glared at his reflection in the mirror and swallowed hard. "I do," she said as she moved away.

Myles walked to the door and held it open. *He had to get out of that room.*

"Then, I guess we'd better get to it…"

THE DRIVE FROM THE HOTEL TO THE CAMP NEAR SERENGETI National Park, where Spencer was said to be studying large animals, was to take nearly ten hours. Myles had suggested they charter a flight, but Jess informed him that the only thing she liked less than small airplanes were small planes in third world countries. Myles hadn't been pleased with this decision so he made a suggestion that he fly while she could drive, a suggestion that did not go over well and in turn led to an intense argument. Needless to say, the ten hours they spent in the car were ten hours in which neither of them spoke to the other. Jess read or pretended to read. He had seen her turn few pages. Myles either stared out the window or studied Jessica—the same way many travelers arrived in Africa to study exotic creatures. While he had a hard time figuring her out, he noted the way the golden tint of her brown hair lit up in the sun, the way she fidgeted with the hem of her dress, and the nervous way she chewed on her bottom lip. He wondered why a woman like her would fly halfway across the world to chase a man. Thankfully, for the both of them, he was a little too smart and a little too polite to pose this question. He predicted the conversation would also not have gone well. And ten hours in a small car where the tension ran high was a little more than he'd bargained for.

Jessica sighed loudly as she looked up from her book and over at him. She shot him a look as though to ask what he was staring at so he turned slightly and refocused his attention out his window.

As he watched the landscape change from farmland to drier desert-looking plains and back again, and he wondered how much further they had yet to go. He checked his watch and considered that it shouldn't be long now. He needed to get out of this car, but more importantly, he needed to get back home and follow up on his lead. *This was it he'd assured himself. He had a feeling about this one.* It both pissed him off and broke his heart that he was here, instead of where he should be, dealing with his own skeletons.

The car pulled off the road into a camp, seemingly in the middle of nowhere. The camp was lined with a dozen or so massive tents along two rows, and a metal building had been erected at the center. The car slowed to a stop and Jessica finally spoke. "I can't believe this is somewhere that Spencer, *my Spencer,* would ever want to stay."

Myles glanced in her direction and then quietly opened the passenger side door. Jess took his extended hand, stepped out in her expensive cocktail dress and pumps. He smiled to himself at how she'd so clearly missed the memo that they were in the middle of the desert in one of the poorest countries on the planet. He leaned back against the car and watched her, half amused, half concerned about how she would fare in those shoes.

She cocked her head to the side and studied his face. "You're not coming?"

He shook his head. "Nah. I'll wait here. Go to the main building and ask for him. I can see you from here."

She started to say something then stopped. Myles watched her start toward the building, unable to walk properly in the heels, no doubt in part due to the terrain, but most likely due to her injuries. He opened the car door and reached into his bag before calling for her. "Hey, Clemens."

She turned. He jogged to catch up and to close the small amount of distance between them. "Here." He held out a pair of women's flip-flops. "We're in Africa. No one cares about fashion here."

Her face gave way to a wide smile as she took them from his hands. As she moved to kick off her heels and Myles took hold of her elbow to steady her. He held up a finger. "Here, let me," he said taking the shoes from her hands and bending down to slip them on her feet. She raised her brow. "You're like a regular ol' boy scout. All prepared and everything. "

Myles glanced up and saw the way she was looking at him, a surprised expression upon her face. "Something like that."

He stood and smoothed her dress a little. "But, honey, you're no Cinderella."

She threw her head back and laughed. "Yeah, tell me about it."

She regained her balance and her face softened even further. "Hey, Myles?"

He waited.

"I think I need you to come with me. Please. It would really mean a lot."

Myles swallowed, pressed his hand to the small of her back, and let her believe she was leading the way.

JESSICA SAT IN THE CENTER OF THE TENT AT A TABLE WHERE one of the attendants had placed her. She meticulously studied her hands. It was a surprisingly ritzy setup, once inside the tents. Certainly not what one would expect to find in the middle of the Serengeti.

Myles stood at the edge of the tent and unsure what to do with himself, pulled a chair out and powered on his cell phone. He checked his email. *Still nothing.*

He and Jess held an on and off, unofficial staring contest until finally, sometime later, a man who Myles guessed to be Spencer Clemens simply by photos he'd seen around the estate, appeared and cautiously yet urgently, made his way over to Jessica.

"What are you doing here?" he asked, alarm written across his face.

He kissed both her cheeks, embraced her, pulled back, and waited.

"We need to talk." She motioned for him to sit down.

Spencer stared at the table then sat down opposite his wife. He glanced at Myles, who stared at his phone.

"You came all this way to talk... Who is *he*?"

Jess looked at Myles, who met her eye and then back at her husband. "He's from the agency. Addison hired him."

Spencer looked his way once more and then back at his wife. "I bet she did."

"Why did you cancel my credit cards?" she started.

"I...I...well, because, darling... anyone can see that you've not been yourself lately."

She furrowed her brow. "And?"

"And because I felt it was for the best."

She leaned back in her chair and furrowed her brow. "You're here," she motioned into thin air around her, "so how would you know what's best?"

Spencer sighed. "I just want you to let me handle things, OK? Just as I've always done. Trust me. You're not homeless, I've made sure you and the children are cared for and that you have what you need, haven't I?"

She waited a long time to respond. Myles considered that maybe she wasn't going to when she finally spoke. "Actually, no. You haven't. We need you home. This isn't right, you being here. I want you to come home with me, Spence."

He shuffled in his seat then rubbed the length of his jaw with one hand. "I... I can't."

She cocked her head. Myles registered surprise in her expression. "Why not?'

"I don't want that life anymore, Jessica."

She swallowed hard. Her palm flew to her chest and she took a deep breath. *Shock*. "What are you saying?"

"I want a divorce. Maybe not right now. But someday—"

Tears had begun falling from her cheeks by this point, but she still managed to cut him off. "I don't understand. Why? Was our marriage... our family really *that* bad? Is it me? The accident? I know I'm not the same person I once was... but I love you, Spencer. And I promise I can be that person again. I can be her again. If you just come home..."

Don't beg, Myles wanted to tell her.

Spencer took a deep breath and held it before letting it out. "I don't know what to say... I just didn't want it anymore. That's why I left. To see if I might change my mind. But I haven't..."

Jessica used her thumbs to wipe the mascara that had begun to smear beneath the tips of her eyelids. She sat up a little straighter. "Is there someone else?"

Spencer looked away. "It's not like that."

"Then tell me. What is it like? Because I just don't understand... I don't understand how you can waltz right out of our lives and halfway across the world without a valid explanation. I mean... remember how mad we were when the Greyers split? You said, Spence... you said that *you* could *never* imagine bailing on your children... on your family, for a job. And you don't even have that. So, tell me, *please*... what reason do you have?"

Spencer pursed his lips and spoke slowly. "I'm gay, Jessica."

～

THE COLOR HAD DRAINED FROM HER FACE. MYLES WAS gauging at which point he might step in, though it wasn't his style, when to her credit, she recovered. "Gay?" she repeated, confused. Myles watched her search her mental catalog for clues.

Her husband couldn't meet her eye. "Yes. Gay."

Jessica shook her head. *She couldn't wrap her head around it. Neither could Myles, if he were being honest.* "I don't understand. How long have you known this?"

He looked up at her then. "My whole life."

"What the fuck, Spencer? What are you saying?" She'd resorted to yelling.

"Calm down, Jessica. Please," Spencer pleaded.

"Calm down? You want me to calm down! You're basically telling me that half of my life has been a total fucking lie…and you want me to calm down?"

"I don't want you to be angry. I want you to understand. And I want you to meet him, actually…"

She deadpanned. "He's here? With you?"

Spencer didn't answer. He didn't have to. His facial expression said it all.

"Oh, my God." Her hand covered her mouth. "I can't believe this is happening—"

Spencer stood. Myles didn't like where this was going and he shifted, ready to get up quickly if he needed to. "There's something else I need to tell you, Jessica—"

Myles watched Jessica brace herself. *She knew.* He watched her pull herself up to a standing position. Myles did the same. He was afraid her legs would give out.

Spencer ran his fingers through his hair quickly and then shoved them in the pockets of his expensive, designer, tailored, jeans. "The money is mostly gone."

Jessica swallowed hard and followed up with a slap no doubt heard round the world.

❧

CHAPTER ELEVEN

Myles firmly placed his hand on his boss's shoulder. "Come on. You two can finish this later."

Jessica crossed her arms and dug her not so literal heels in. "I'm not done."

Spencer rubbed at the red blotchy skin on his face.

Myles looked from Jessica to her husband and back at her before speaking. "Jess, I said let's go."

"He's right. I think you need to go, Jessica. We can talk about this later... when you've calmed down." Spencer eyed Myles then. "Where are you staying?"

Myles shook his head just slightly and didn't reply. Instead, he grasped Jess by the wrist and practically hauled her to the awaiting car.

"I'm not ready to go," she whispered quietly as he opened the car door and shooed her in. Myles locked the door, closed it, and hustled around to the other side.

He climbed in and addressed the driver. "Take us to the nearest airport, please."

Jess placed her head in her hands, hunched forward, and rested them on her knees. Myles placed his hand on her back and left it there as she sobbed. She would rock gently, pause to catch her breath, and then continue sobbing. It lasted for the entirety of the hour and a half long trip to the small airport. "Wait here for a half hour, and if we're not back, you can go," Myles said handing the driver a twenty once he'd pulled to the curb and stopped.

He nudged Jessica. "Come on. We have to get out now."

She slouched down in the seat and shook her head. Myles pulled a tissue from his bag and handed it to her. "I can't leave you here while I run in." He looked in the direction of the driver from the corner of his eye and back at her. "I don't trust it's safe."

She blew her nose. "I'm not getting on a plane."

Myles exhaled loudly. "Listen, we were scheduled to stay at the camp overnight… There's no way it's safe to make the ten-hour trip back to Nairobi in the dark." He paused and continued his voice firm. "Things don't work that way here, Jessica."

Her eyes widened. "But I'm terrified of flying. You don't understand…"

Myles opened his bag partially and pointed to a vial of pills. He nodded. "We're prepared for that."

She cocked her head to the side and then reluctantly, took his hand. He sighed, opened the car door, and led her out.

"I'm sorry, Mister," the attendant said with a heavy accent. "All flights out for today have already departed."

Myles pinched the bridge of his nose and took a deep breath. *He should've prepared for this.* He eyed Jessica, who had found a seat and was curled into a ball. *Goddamn it. He'd seen easier situations in the Navy.*

He produced a hundred dollar bill from his pocket and showed it to the man. "There's nothing you can do?"

The man frowned. "Wind advisory today, we can't fly anymore. Not up to me. Up to God." He pointed upward. "Sorry."

Myles shoved the money back into his pocket and made his way over to Jessica. "You're in luck."

She stared blankly out the window at the tarmac.

"We're staying here tonight." He eyed the men gathered outside holding machine guns.

Her eyes followed his. "Here? You mean in this town? Or here, here."

"I mean here. In the airport. It's safer that way."

"You're kidding, right?"

He looked at her and offered a small smile. "No, I'm afraid not."

To this, she simply shrugged. "Some luck," she finally said. The fight, or what little she'd ever had, was now clearly gone.

MYLES DIDN'T SLEEP AT ALL THAT NIGHT. INSTEAD, HE watched his boss swallow a few pills, and then toss and turn while mostly staring into space—and also not sleep. He let her be. There was nothing either of them could do or say that would make the situation suck any less.

Finally, sometime in the middle of the night, she sat straight up and turned to him. "What would you do if you were me?"

Myles didn't look her way. "I can't say. Because I'm not."

She scoffed. "Improvise."

He sat up and turned her way. "I guess I'd move on. I mean, what else *can* you do?"

"I just can't wrap my head around it. I've searched my

brain this way and that way... and nothing." She shrugged and wiped a stray tear. "I never saw this coming."

Myles swallowed. "It happens."

She frowned. "I don't believe him... about the money."

He studied her face. "You shouldn't..."

She snapped back and then her expression relaxed. "What do you mean?"

"I just don't think he's telling you the whole truth about it... but look, this really isn't my business."

"Well, you're here. So that sort of makes you an accomplice."

Myles shook his head. "It makes me your employee."

She inhaled sharply and then let it out slowly. "I see."

HE SHOULDN'T HAVE SAID THAT, HE THOUGHT AS HE RECALLED the way her face fell. It was an asshole thing to say, and he knew it the moment the words danced on the tip of his tongue. *But what else could he do?* She was getting too close. They couldn't be friends because Myles didn't have friends. *More importantly, he didn't want friends.*

These thoughts troubled him for the rest of the night. The following morning, he understood his predicament a little better. According to his SEAL training, there were times in life where one had to do what needed to be done—what the situation required, not what one wanted. So, exactly forty-five minutes before their flight was to take off for Nairobi where they would stay over another night and then head back to the States, Myles handed her two Xanax, against his better judgment. This seemed to relax her, but as the plane ascended, Jessica tightly gripped his thigh just above his knee. Every instinct in his body wanted to remove her hand and yet Myles couldn't make himself do it. He eyed her white knuckles and willed himself not to give in to the fear. Finally, her hand relaxed as she looked up and noticed his face.

Jess laughed. "I'm sorry. Did that hurt?"

He swallowed, picked up her hand, and placed it back in her own lap.

"Wow. So touchy," she slurred. And then she perked up. "Myles, I need a favor. I mean… I know you're here as my employee, not my friend. I'm sorry I let those lines blur. I'll pay you, of course..."

He raised his brow. *It was as though she'd seen right through every ounce of guilt he'd ever had.*

"I can borrow from my parents… until this is all sorted out."

Ouch. She wasn't the only one who'd blurred the lines. He regained his composure. "Of course, you can."

"What is that supposed to mean?"

He glanced out the window and then back at her. "Nothing. I'm sorry I said it."

"Well, it's just that I'm probably never coming back to Africa and this isn't exactly the memory I want to have of it."

Myles frowned. "And…?"

"And, I want an adventure…"

"I'd say this has been an adventure."

She slapped his shoulder. "You know what I mean."

He was afraid he had a clue. "You're not acting like a woman scorned."

She threw her head back and laughed. "Yeah, well, no doubt thanks to your Xanax mixed with my Xanax. Plus, there's plenty of time for that…"

Myles deadpanned. "You weren't supposed to have Xanax on you. What I had *was* yours."

He felt her watching carefully as he fumed. "How many did you take?"

Jess grinned. "Just three…but I borrowed a few bottles of vodka from the mini-bar, too."

He turned in his seat before looking over his shoulder. "I'm done babysitting, Jessica. You're a fucking child."

Her expression turned devious. "So, I take it that's a no?"

Myles turned back and stared out the window. He was running out of patience. And nothing good had ever come from that happening.

"Sit on the bed," he ordered once back at the hotel where he'd taken her to his room so that he could keep an eye on her.

He'd caught her off guard. "Sit." He demanded once again.

She eyed the chair then reluctantly took a seat.

Myles paced. "I'm going to tell you something and it doesn't leave this room. Do you understand what I'm saying?"

She nodded slowly.

"Say it," he said, his voice hard. He lowered his voice and started again. "I need to hear you say it."

"All right. I pinky promise. It doesn't leave this room."

He swallowed and paced some more before stopping abruptly. "I have… I had a daughter."

"You—?"

Myles held up his hand and cut her off. He paused then sat on the edge of the bed, facing her and met her gaze head on. "Let me finish. I was married… once. We had a daughter, and when she was three, she died. As if that isn't fucked up enough… I didn't know… I didn't even make it home in time for the funeral. I didn't even find out she was dead for eight days. *Eight fucking days.* I was on a mission that couldn't be interrupted, they'd later said. But the truth is that's how it always was. I was a Navy SEAL, which basically meant that I was always gone. And that was pretty much how my life was. I did what I felt I needed to do, what I felt was best for me. And, you know what? It cost me. I wasn't there when my child got sick, and I wasn't there when they put her in the ground. People like to say that I was doing my duty—but you know what? That's fucking bullshit. My family and my child were *my* duties. And I failed at it. I failed at being a husband and I failed at being a father. I basically failed the whole mission. After she died, it was clearer than it had been before, and so my wife left. She left our home, she took her things... and she *just* left. By the time I got back, she was already gone. I haven't seen her since. Eight days. It's amazing how your whole life can just disappear in eight days."

He shook his head and sighed. "Three months later, I received divorce papers and a letter. And that was that."

Jess swallowed. "Oh, my God. I didn't know... I'm sorry."

He shrugged. "You're probably wondering why I'm telling you this..."

She shook her head slightly.

"Well, I'm telling you because it's something you need to hear. And I guess... it's something I need to say. I don't have many friends at this point, and if I did have one, you'd be the closest thing to it. You're taking your life, Jessica... you're taking your children for granted. Do you have any idea what it's like to lose a child? I'm going to go out on a limb and guess not. Well... let me tell you... a part of you fucking dies. Nothing and I mean *nothing* is ever the same." Myles took a deep breath, let it out, and continued. "I can see that you're hurting. That your life hasn't turned out like you thought it would... but guess what? No one's life does. I see clearly what's coming for you, and it's either another overdose or losing your kids... and either way, *they* lose. Do you have any idea what I would give to have a second chance? To have a tiny bit of what you have. Your life isn't perfect. That's obvious. But have you stopped to notice how your kids look at you? Have you considered them in any of this? Because I have."

Jess stared at the floor. "I'm sorry. I didn't know," she said and then she stood and went to him. "You're right. And I guess the answer is no. Well, yes and no. I know I've been selfish. But I just don't feel anything. I'm numb... and it's been this way for so long now that I don't know what to do about it. I can't stop... it just feels *too* big. Too far beyond what I'm capable of. And now, I come here... and there's this to deal with. "

He turned slightly to face her. "I get it, but there's a lot to lose in your position. You must see that, right?"

Jessica leaned in and brushed his bangs from his eyes. "What are you suggesting I do?"

Myles scooted backward just an inch on the bed. *He knew that look.* "I have a feeling what you're thinking, and it isn't the answer... you need to sober up, Jessica."

She swallowed hard. "I'm not that high." She closed the gap between them. "Just once. I need to feel something... "

He inched backward again. "That sounds like a bad movie line. And I'm afraid it doesn't work that way."

She gave him a hard look. "Au contraire. I've seen you with your women."

Myles considered how she'd cornered him. "I can't have sex with you and then stick around. *I* don't work that way."

Jessica cocked her head to the side. "What if we made a deal? *I* get clean... *you* stick around."

Myles snorted. "That's not a deal... that's a relationship."

She bit her lip and then smiled slyly. *It was driving him crazy the way she was looking at him and he was afraid she knew it.* "No. It's a business arrangement."

Myles knew this was a terrible idea and yet he leaned in and kissed her anyway. *Just once. He needed to know what it felt like to give in.*

She let him kiss her until he seemed satisfied, and then she pulled away slowly and studied his face. "So, I take it, that's *not* a no?"

Myles searched her eyes. "It's a maybe…"

Her face lit up and she cocked her head, curious. "A maybe based on what?"

He smiled. "How good the sex is."

She swallowed hard, nodded, and raised her brow. "You should know then that it's been awhile…"

Myles leaned closer, grabbed her hips, and lowered her backward onto the bed. "Yeah, well, it's sort of like riding a bike…" He whispered as he raised her arms over her head and held them there. He trailed kisses down her neck and then back up again until he reached her ear. "You don't forget…"

She practically purred as he let his other hand trail down her thigh and up her dress. He paused and reached for his wallet, removed a condom, and then slipped her panties off and undid his pants. He never took his eyes from hers. He was almost certain she'd call his bluff and back out, which would've been fine because this level of intimacy was too much for him in every sense, but when she raised her brow as though to ask what he was waiting for, he forced himself to level up and answered the unspoken question by plunging into her. Hard. She gasped and gripped his shirt, then released her grip, and dug her nails into his back. Myles didn't slow the intensity of his thrusts. He didn't make love to her the way he probably should have. He fucked her. This was what the situation called for, he realized, whether it was right or not. He was rougher than he'd intended, but a part of him didn't care. And she didn't seem to mind too much either.

CHAPTER TWELVE

"What did we just do?" Jessica asked as they lay there tangled up in each other.

"We fucked."

"*Yeah.* We did." She swallowed, her mouth dry, her legs trembling, those distant and yet familiar trembles she had so missed. "I haven't been fucked like that in… well, forever."

"That's a shame," he remarked as he sat up and handed her a bottle of water after twisting the cap off.

She sipped the water, handed it back to him, and then stood up slowly, straightening her dress.

Myles look confused. "What are you doing?"

"Going back to my room."

He furrowed his brow.

"You don't want to talk or cuddle or anything."

She eyed him, and then shook her head slowly. "No. Do you?"

He smiled. "No."

"Good," she said turning toward the door.

"Good," he agreed standing and making his way over to her.

Myles put his hand against the door so she couldn't open it. He ran his lips along the back of her neck. "Hey, Jessica," he said, his voice low, before resuming his trail along the back of her neck ending just behind her ear.

Chills. She froze instantly.

"Can I call you?" he whispered.

She smiled to herself. "Maybe."

He returned the smile, released the door, and held it open.

JESS DREW A BATH AND SOAKED IN IT UNTIL SHE SHRIVELED UP and the water turned cold. She was beyond tired. She was sore and spent. She'd hoped for sleep, but instead, found she only tossed and turned in her bed. A drink would help, but she found the mini bar empty. *No doubt it was Myles' doing.* He also held her pills, and though she desperately craved one, the last thing she wanted was to have to ask for it at a time like this. *What had she just done?* Her husband was gay. *Gay.* She did her best to think back over her marriage, searching for signs that he was interested in the opposite sex, but nothing apparent stuck out. *It was too soon.* She couldn't go there. She was still in shock. The news and the sting, both still too raw.

In the meantime, a one-night stand or two couldn't hurt. Sure, she had crossed a few too many lines by having sex with her employee, but, on the other hand, it made her feel something that she hadn't felt in a long time. *Desired.* As she dozed off, she wondered how this had become her life. How she'd ended up halfway across the world with an essential stranger dishing out her drugs and a husband that no longer wanted the life they'd had. A husband who'd not only been living a lie, but had taken the last little bit of hope she'd had when he informed her their money was gone. Whether this were true or not, only time would tell.

One thing was certain though—Jessica realized that she had to get her life together and fast.

THE PHONE BUZZING JARRED JESS FROM HER SLEEP.

"Hello," she whispered in the dark.

"Can I come over?" the deep voice asked.

"What time is it?"

"Four in the afternoon."

She sighed. "If… you bring me a pill or two."

The door clicked and Myles entered her room.

Jess pulled the covers over her head. "Jesus. I forgot you had a key."

"Here." He placed the pills and a bottle of water on the bedside table.

Jessica sat up and studied his face. "How did she die?"

Myles froze. He winced and then sat down on the bed beside her. "Jessica— let me be clear about something. That part of my life is not open for discussion. It isn't something I want to revisit."

She grabbed the two pills and tossed them back. "Got it."

"About earlier," he said, nodding toward his room. "I'm sorry. It shouldn't have happened."

Her mouth gaped open but she quickly recovered. "You woke me up to tell me this?"

He stood and began straightening the room. "No, it was time for your medication."

"You know what, Myles? You can hide all you want to… but you're no less fucked up than I am," Jess muttered, throwing the half empty water bottle at his back.

He turned, picked the water bottle up, and placed it

firmly back on her bedside table. He turned to go then stopped mid-stride. "Who's hiding?" he called over his shoulder. "I'm right next door," he said as though it were an invitation and then let the door slam.

OLD HABITS DIE HARD. IT WAS ALWAYS BETTER TO STOP THESE things before they started, he knew. Myles studied the horizon out the window. He was involved enough as it was, and he really didn't need this in his life to begin with. That woman was a train wreck waiting to happen and he wanted off the ride. The problem was he liked her. The trouble was she liked him.

Myles sat that way lost in thought until he heard the key card swipe click and his door open. *Motherfucker.* He guessed it wasn't the cleaning lady.

But he didn't turn to check.

"I'll pay you," she said, slurring her words.

Myles let out a long sigh. *Good God.*

He kept his back to her. "For sex?"

"Not for sex. That's illegal. And skanky... and desperate—"

"I get your point," he spat, cutting her off. "You need to cut back on the pills. I'm no doctor, but they're prescribing you more than you need—by at least half."

"I know," she replied flatly.

He turned halfway. He hadn't expected that answer.

"What I meant was I'll pay you to help me get clean. I know... *I know* that we slept together and that changes things, but I'm also a little more perceptive than you think about your method of operation. I know your style. You're in and then you're out. *Pun intended.* Now, I get that you may not be emotionally prepared for the work that this job calls for... but you see—the thing is, I could really use a friend right now. And I'm no psychologist or anything… but it appears that we both could…"

"Don't psycho-analyze me, Jessica."

"Fine. But can I at least ask you a couple of questions?"

"No."

"Myles—please. Play along… just halfway, that's all I'm asking."

She placed her hands on her hips and waited. He studied her face and suddenly, hated himself for the way he was treating her. He relented. "Shoot."

"How many women have you had sex with in the past year?"

"I don't know. Why—?"

She cocked her head to the side. *Challenging him.* "I think you do know."

He sighed. "One hundred and sixty-three."

Her mouth flew open. "That's almost—"

Myles was quick to cut her off. "I know how many it is."

Jessica swallowed. "Wow." He watched as she shifted to balance her weight on her stronger leg. *He wanted to go to her, but he didn't.* "Do you still have contact with any of them?"

He was done with this conversation. *Who was she to say whether he was or wasn't emotionally prepared, anyway? She didn't even know him.* "No. I like sex, all right. No strings attached—sex. It's pretty simple, actually. I'm safe… I get tested regularly. A number is just a number. So, I have a big appetite?" Myles shrugged. "I don't see what's so wrong with that…"

"I think you do."

"This isn't about me, Jessica. My life is my life and I'm not hurting anyone."

She glared at him for a few moments, waiting for him to say something else. And when she realized he wasn't going to, she added, "Keep telling yourself that," and walked out.

MYLES DRESSED, LACED UP HIS SHOES, AND HEADED TO THE hotel gym. He figured a run would clear his mind. But after spending an hour pounding the treadmill left him feeling no more clarity than when he'd started, he knew just where he needed to go.

He headed straight for Jess's room only to find it empty. *Shit. His one job was to watch her and he hadn't even done that well. This wasn't that hard and here he was failing again.* He dialed her cell. *No answer.* Myles took the elevator down knowing exactly where he'd find her all the while praying that she hadn't yet slipped in deeper than either of them could handle. Sure enough, there she was all fancied up, sitting at the bar, legs crossed, in a pencil skirt and six inch heels. *Waiting. What he didn't understand was how a woman recovering from her injuries could manage in heels like that.*

Myles took a seat in the empty chair next to hers. She looked over at him and then away.

"I'm sorry." He eyed the glass in her hand. "But please don't do this."

"*You're* sorry?" she mocked, nursing her cocktail.

Myles took the drink from her hand and placed it on the bar. Jess shot him a go to hell look but didn't move to pick the glass back up. "I know your personal life is in shambles. I know you're in pain, most of the time. Believe me, I know. But the way you're managing it is all wrong. You need to let yourself feel the pain. Sit with it a while. Stop doing this to yourself."

She shifted, uncrossed, and then re-crossed her legs. "Is that how you do it?"

"No."

"I didn't think so."

"But I'm willing to work on it if you are. I've given your

proposition some thought… and I've decided I'd like to see it through if you're still game."

She smirked. "Oh, yeah?"

He placed his hand on the back of her chair and leaned in. "With a few minor concessions on your part, I think we can make it work."

She studied her half-empty glass, and then traced her finger around the rim. "And those would be?"

"There are a few. But, for starters, you need to understand what pain is. And how to live with it. You're capable of more than you think…"

Jess raised her brow. "What makes you so sure?"

"Instinct," he said as he stood and reached for her hand. "And the fact that I've always liked a good challenge."

She smiled. *That, he was certainly in for.* She pulled away.

He leaned in closer. "This isn't going to be easy, you know?" he whispered. She narrowed her brow and considered the implications of what he'd said.

Myles didn't wait for a response. He simply grinned, grabbed her arm just above the elbow, and led her out of the bar and back to his room. Pain was a given, she'd just realized. And sometimes, you just needed to give into it—no matter what form it showed up in.

CHAPTER THIRTEEN

M yles paced the length of his hotel room and checked his watch. Thankful he'd gotten her out of that bar, he realized there were just twelve more hours, and they could get the hell out of this place. The hotel walls were beginning to close in on him, and he had never looked more forward to getting back to the States. Jess stood looking at him, clearly a little unsure what to do with herself. He punched the code into the small safe, then handed Jessica her next dose of medication and walked to the sink to wash his face. He paused and studied her reflection instead. How did someone let a woman like that get away, he wondered to himself? The blessing and the curse was that he knew the answer. No matter how hard you tried, you could never be what they needed. Never enough. A woman like that, and this he knew for sure, would consume you. She'd eat you whole if you let her. But how could you not?

Myles watched the relief play across her face as the pills slid down her throat. He noticed the length of her neck as she tossed her head back. It was all he could do not to go to her, to wrap his hand around her neck, and to do things to her that he was fairly certain hadn't been done in quite a while. There was going to be something magical about this one, he understood, as much as he tried to fight it.

On the other hand, he had an addict on his hands, and while a part of him knew he couldn't keep doing this, he couldn't just walk out either. Things had to change, and the way it looked from where he stood, both of them were about to find out just how much they could take. He could do this, he assured himself. *Part of loving someone was giving them what they need.* He'd planned it out—the next step was to place a call to the agency and set everything up. But first, she'd have to agree.

"Have a seat," he ordered catching her eye in the mirror.

Jess frowned. "You want to talk? I had something else in mind..."

"Sit down, Jessica."

She plopped down in the chair, crossed her arms, and stared out the window.

Defiance. She was a natural. "If we're going to do this... *if* I'm going to stay, then you need to know the rules."

She smirked. *The rules.*

He lowered his voice. "This isn't funny."

Jess met his eyes, narrowed her gaze, and then looked away.

"Sit up and have some respect. And look me in the eye," Myles demanded.

She frowned but did as he'd asked. "What is wrong with you?"

"This isn't a joke. We either do this my way or it won't work."

She kicked off her heels, leaned forward, and rubbed at her toes.

Myles backed away putting some distance between the two of them. "Do you know what re-socialization is, Jessica?"

She looked up, clearly caught off guard, and shook her head. "What?"

"There are generally four types of training techniques used in the re-socialization process. Brutalization, classical conditioning, operant conditioning, and role modeling. I realize this probably means nothing to you right now, but it's what I need you to agree to—if *I'm* going to agree to stick around."

She tilted her head. "Brutalization? That sounds crazy."

"It is crazy." He eyed her intently. "But it works."

Myles sat down on the bed, leaned forward, and rested his arms on his knees. "It's in part how they break you down in the military."

She swallowed. "And you want me to agree to this, why?"

"You need to get sober. And I need to keep you safe in the meantime."

"You mean keep yourself safe?"

He shrugged slightly. "That, too."

"What exactly does this brutalization entail?"

"Mostly, what it implies."

"And what if I can't do it?"

He inhaled slowly and let it out. "Then I can't stick around."

Jessica sighed and leaned back in her chair. "You do understand that I'm already in quite a predicament because I gave my power away, right?"

"This is different. It's about getting your power back, in a way that serves you. It doesn't involve money. There are clearly written, agreed upon rules from the start. And of course, this sort of arrangement requires complete trust and open, direct communication."

Her eyes widened then relaxed. "Myles. Myles. Myles… what you're asking is absurd. What I don't need right now is someone taking anything else from me or telling me how to be. Enough of that has already occurred. My life is a complete fucking mess…"

"That's one way to look at it, sure. But this is also giving your life back to you in a way that prepares you to deal with it. Something you haven't been doing a very good job of—to put it mildly. It's no different from Basics in the U.S. Military."

"So… you're offering me boot camp?"

He considered her analogy for a moment and smiled. "With sex added."

She glared at him. "Well, when you put it like that…"

"Look, Jessica… to put it in the simplest of terms, you need to get sober. And more importantly, to get your life together. I need to be able to handle being close to someone again in a way that makes sense for me. Both of these things require a considerable amount of effort and a fair amount of trust."

She smiled, and then let it fade. "How much sex are we talking?"

He leaned back and eyed her from head to toe, his gaze stopping on hers. "As much as you can handle."

Jessica raised her brow, apparently satisfied with his answer. "I want to read the rules first."

He let his eyes light up, but just briefly. *This was going to be fun.* "Fair enough."

JESSICA STARED AT HER REFLECTION IN THE MIRROR AS MYLES stood behind her. She watched as he unzipped her skirt and then took her hand as she stepped out of it. He unbuttoned her blouse, one by one, taking his time. *Too much time.* The rules could wait just a bit, he'd said.

"Do you trust me?" he asked as he unfastened her bra and ran his hands over her body.

She nodded, but when she met his eye, he firmly grabbed her neck and ordered her to focus on her own reflection.

Once she had, and he was satisfied, he used his foot to gently splay her legs, a hips' distance apart. "I want to hear you say it."

Jess exhaled. "I trust you."

"It's important that you do as I say. If there's something you don't want to do or if you want to stop, at any time, just say so."

She met his eyes again. He leaned forward and took her chin between his fingers and squeezed. Hard. "Eyes straight ahead."

Myles paused for a second to make sure she followed, and then carefully traced his fingers down the side of her body until he reached the scars. He stopped there and then ran his fingers back up again, before trailing back down once more. He lingered over each scar, tracing them one by one. "You're so beautiful," he whispered.

She looked away. "The scars don't help any."

Jessica froze as his hand landed a swift blow across her ass. She flinched, met his gaze, and then reflexively rubbed at the sting. Myles shook his head slightly, but enough that she noticed, then removed her hand, and firmly placed it back on the sink. "Your scars make you interesting."

She swallowed.

"I want *you* to say it," he ordered.

Jess exhaled letting every last bit of air out that she'd had in her lungs. Another blow. Tears stung at the corner of her eyes.

She watched him raise his hand to strike again. "I said say it."

Another blow, this time to the other cheek. *Never in the same spot.*

"Fine! Okay... my scars make me interesting."

He looked directly at her, then knelt, and slowly began kissing her ass, sucking and massaging the welts with both his tongue and his hands relentlessly until she practically melted into him. Jess held her breath. *It was too much. She couldn't handle this.*

"Do you need more?"

Her body and her mind told her yes even though her heart wanted to make it stop. She wanted to say as much. Instead, she let her eyes answer for her.

"Say, 'I need more, please.'"

Her throat had suddenly gone dry. She swallowed hard before eventually getting the words out. "I need more, please."

Myles stood, positioned himself behind her, pulled her face back toward him, forcing her to arch her back, just enough to where he knew it wouldn't hurt. He bit her earlobe, gently sucking it between his teeth, then again a little harder before releasing it and whispering in her ear, "Now, eyes straight ahead. You're going to watch me show you how beautiful you are." He pushed into her, slowly, and then all at once. And this time, he was pleasantly surprised to find that she didn't push back.

∾

CHAPTER FOURTEEN

Jessica awoke to an unfamiliar ringing sound. She rubbed at her eyes, rolled toward the edge of the bed, and fumbled in the dark before grabbing the receiver. The operator on the other end of the line informed her that a Mr. Clemens was in the hotel lobby and had asked that she meet him downstairs. *What in the hell was he doing here? She was both surprised, and yet not surprised.*

Jess quickly rose, washed her face, wrapped a hotel robe around her pajamas, and headed for the elevator. Anxious, she wondered what her husband could possibly want showing up at her hotel at five in the morning. She cautiously considered for a second that perhaps this had all just been a very bad joke. *Maybe he'd come to his senses and was coming back to her. Maybe it was all a lie. His way of testing her.*

As the elevator doors opened and Jess stepped out, she spotted her husband immediately. He was well-dressed in a suit and tie, just like the Spencer she knew and loved. The only thing different was their location and the knowledge he'd imparted upon her that everything, everything, was different. She noticed the way his expression changed as he met her gaze. He stood and ushered her over and Jess realized that she stood frozen just inside the elevator doors. She made her way over to where he'd been sitting and stopped. From afar, he'd looked familiar, but upon further inspection, up close, there was something noticeably different about him, which Jess couldn't quite place.

"What are you doing here?"

Spencer smiled despondently and motioned at the oversized chair opposite him.

Jess eyed the chair and then sat and folded her hands in her lap.

"I didn't want you to fly out of here without getting a few things settled."

"So you're still gay?" she retorted, the anger unexpectedly creeping upward.

Spencer looked himself up and down before glaring at the floor. "I'm still gay." He chewed his lip before continuing. "I understand you're angry and I'm sorry, Jessica. I know this isn't what you expected to find coming here. To tell you the truth, I'm not really sure what to say—"

Jess cocked her head to the side. Her chest tightened. "Why are you staring at the floor?" she demanded.

He met her eyes hesitantly. "I'm not sure where to look."

She motioned at the vicinity of her head. "This would be a good place."

"I'm sorry. I don't know what you want me to say, and I'm not sure where to start. This isn't easy…"

"Well, you could start by telling me why you deceived me for all these years. And finish by explaining just what happened to our money."

Spencer nodded. *He'd expected this.* "I didn't mean for it to happen this way… I didn't mean to hurt you. But when you live a lie for so long, Jess, it eats away at you. It consumes you. And soon, there are lies, and then more lies, until all of a sudden everything you know is a lie. It's self-perpetuating like that."

Jess swallowed back the bile she felt rising in her throat. "How could you do this to me? To our kids?"

"It's not something I did. It's not even something I wanted to do. It's who I am."

"You know what, Spence—you're a coward. You've lied to me for years. You led me on. You let me believe that you loved me... that we were in this together. But the truth was you were never *really* in it to begin with."

Spencer studied her face and then looked away. "I did love you, Jessica. I mean, I do love you. Just not in the way that you need..."

She brushed the hair away from her face. "That's a fucking understatement if I've ever heard one."

He shifted. "About the money—the thing is, I made some bad investments. All of the money in our shared accounts is gone..." Her husband eyed her sullenly before looking away. "I'm sorry, and I promise to pay every penny of your portion back to you. But... I didn't touch your inheritance... your dad put some pretty thick red tape in place around that."

Jess shook her head. "Well, thank God for that."

Spencer swallowed hard. "And that's in part why I came... I'm..." He paused to run his hand through his hair and then continued. "I'm in trouble, Jess. That's why I'm here. Well, partly... why I'm here."

She frowned. "What kind of trouble?"

Her husband brushed her off with the wave of his hand. "Nothing major. Just made a few bad deals, is all." He paused and slowed his pace. "Listen, I need to borrow some money from your trust. I need you to talk to our accountant and have them transfer it over... I swear to you I'll pay you back in full with interest."

Jess rubbed at her temples. "I don't—"

She was cut off when a firm hand grabbed her shoulder. Jess turned to see Myles towering over her. Spencer stood abruptly and held out his hand. Myles glared at his hand until Spencer retracted it and promptly stuffed it in his pocket. Spencer studied Jessica and then looked back at Myles. "Well, hey, I guess I'd better be going and let you two get on with it."

He nodded at Myles then turned to his wife. "Well, have a safe flight—I'll give you a ring once you've landed. The accountant will probably be calling too, just a heads up."

Jessica stood and tried to steady herself. She shifted her weight from one leg to another.

Myles cleared his throat and placed his hand firmly on the small of Jess's back.

Spencer leaned in then and kissed Jessica's cheek. She didn't move to resist. "Give the kids my love. I'll call them here in a bit."

Jess nodded then watched him stride out of the hotel lobby and make his way out through the automatic doors. Tears silently ran down her cheeks as she watched the man she'd loved for so long, the man she'd committed her life to, the man who held her hand nervously as she pushed their children out into the world, walk as confidently as ever right out of her life without even once looking back.

Myles eyed her from head to toe, and back up again stopping at her leg. "You hurting?"

"Something like that."

He straightened his back and then knelt down. "Climb on."

Jess wiped her tears with both hands before getting what he was asking of her. "I'm not getting on your back!" she scoffed.

Myles stood and turned, his eyes pouring into her. "Fine… but just so you know… you're passing up one of the best piggyback rides you would have ever received… that's a lot to pass up."

She shot him a look of skepticism and hesitated. She looked around the lobby not yet bustling with people and then back at him. "Fine," she relented.

Myles knelt down once more and let her climb on. He stood, adjusted her position, and headed toward the elevator. He surprised her when he turned for the stairwell. "I wasn't wrong, was I?"

Jess furrowed her brow. "Why are we taking the stairs?"

"I could use the energy expenditure I refrained from letting out on your husband's face."

"That's not very nice," she huffed.

"Yeah, well…"

Jess inhaled deeply then laid her cheek against his shoulder and exhaled. "I'm not saying you were right… but you weren't exactly wrong either."

She smiled to herself. It hurt like hell, both her leg and the situation. But there was something other than the pain this time. She wouldn't exactly say it was hope, but perhaps the longing for something more. *What a ride this life is, she considered.* And to think she hadn't even taken her pills yet.

MYLES ENTERED JESS'S HOTEL ROOM, THIS TIME WITHOUT warning. *Something she was going to have to get used to.* He surveyed the room and threw his hands up in the air. "Why aren't you packed? We need to go."

He handed her pills to her. "We need to fix this problem."

Jess tossed them back, and then looked at him straight-faced before she released her wet hair from the towel it was wrapped in and tossed it on the floor. She adjusted and tightened the towel she still had wrapped around her body before addressing him again. "Jeez. Relax. We have time... I needed a shower..."

Myles glared at her. "Pick it up."

Jess looked down at the towel and gave him her best 'you've got to be kidding me' face.

"Yes," he said, acknowledging she'd gotten it right. "The towel. I said pick it up."

Jess narrowed her brow and met his gaze head on. "What is wrong with you?"

Myles closed the gap between them and positioned himself directly in front of her, his eyes boring into hers. "This isn't your house, and even if it was, someone has to pick that up. Starting today, that *someone* is going to be you."

Jess started to speak then hesitated choosing her words carefully knowing this was about so much more than either of them was readily willing to admit. She stepped backward then turned to face the large window. "I don't see what the big deal is... it's just a towel. That's what the maids are paid for, to clean up. It's sort of job security."

Myles stepped forward and grabbed the portion of the towel wrapped around her at her chest and yanked. Jess turned to look over her shoulder, confused by his anger.

"Bend over," he ordered.

Jess rolled her eyes. "Fine. I'll pick up the damned towel."

As she turned and stepped forward to lean over and reach for the towel, Myles caught her by the waist with one arm. He lifted her slightly off the floor and hugged her body firmly into his to prevent her from moving, and walked the few steps to the bed where he deftly and firmly placed her stomach down. He placed one hand on the small of her back to hold her in place. *She didn't resist.* Swiftly, he raised the hand that gripped the wet towel she'd been wearing and swatted her hard against her backside with it. As it struck her, Jess sucked in all the air she could into her lungs and held it there. He paused and waited just briefly as he watch her fingers tangle and grip the sheets. *She knew what was coming.* He reared his arm back and then playfully let the towel trail along her ass and thighs before picking it up again and slapping hard, this time against her thighs. Satisfied then, he dropped the towel and carefully flipped her over. Towering over her, he lowered himself down, his eyes on hers. He leaned forward, took her bottom lip between his teeth, and tugged. Jess swallowed hard as he released her lip, and then kissed her softly. "The first welt was for assuming someone else would take responsibility for your shit. And the second was for rolling your eyes and disobeying my order." He studied her face, looking pained, then reached down, and pinched her nipple hard. "If we weren't pressed for time, which has only been further exaggerated by your carelessness and defiance, I would fuck you good enough that the sting you feel across your ass right now would be mild in comparison to the pleasure you'd feel by begging me for release. Never forget, Jessica, your actions—they not only hinder your pleasure, but the pleasure of others, as well."

Jess propped herself up on her elbows causing him to fall backward slightly. "I haven't agreed to your rules… or your agreement yet."

Myles brushed the back of his hand across her chest and then down her stomach. He ran one finger over her clit and then slipped it inside her. "Riddle me this. Did you ask me to stop when I laid you over the bed and swatted that sweet little ass of yours? Most importantly, did you *want* me to stop?"

Jess froze, swallowed hard as he slipped another finger in. She shook her head, ever so slightly, but enough that they both understood.

He grinned and removed his fingers. "Then, by default,

you agreed. We shouldn't let that happen again though, should we?"

Jess shook her head, stood, tangled her fingers around the roots of his hair, twisted, and yanked his face toward hers. She kissed him hard. "How do *you* like it?"

He pulled back just slightly, his hair still tangled in her fingers and eyed her naked body. "I quite like it." He smiled.

Frustrated beyond what mere words could convey, she released his hair, dressed, and hurriedly packed her things.

Damn, he was good.

CHAPTER FIFTEEN

J ess hadn't been back home with her children for more
than twenty-four hours before Myles handed her the
note that would forever change the course of her life.
Looking back, she realizes that the course had likely already
changed sometime before that, but this was the event that set
all others in motion. She carefully unfolded the note without
failing to notice that it was written on her very own
stationery. An irony that wasn't altogether lost on her. *At
least someone was writing.*

DEAR JESSICA,

AS PER OUR PRIOR DISCUSSION, I'D LIKE TO BE A PART OF
helping to get your life back on the right track. I promised
you a list of rules regarding the 're-socialization project' I
proposed and they are as follows:

   1. You must consent to the detox process and refrain
from using all drugs, including alcohol, and remain clean at

all times—participating in Narcotics Anonymous Meetings once a week for the duration of the program.

2. You must adhere to all methods of treatment both the doctor and I set forth, including but not limited to: a healthy diet, exercise and other various means of promoting well-being.

3. You must maintain complete open and honest communication with me at all times.

4. You pledge that you will mend fences with those who have been affected by your actions as a user.

5. You must agree to write daily.

If you consent to the above terms, you need to be ready to leave first thing in the morning. We will be away for approximately three weeks, give or take. The regular staff and your mother will care for the children. She'll bring them to visit toward the latter end of the stay. Addison is aware of the situation and together, we have put a physician in place that will assist with the detoxification process. I need you to make sure that you are ready to commit as I believe we both realize this will not be a fun journey.

But know that if you do not agree to the above terms, I cannot stay on.

SINCERELY,
  Myles

JESS FOLDED THE NOTE AND PLACED IT BACK ON HER BEDSIDE table. The way she saw it there was little choice in the matter. She realized she needed to get clean and in the process, sort through a whole host of situations in her life. She would have to begin the process of dissolving her marriage, of getting her life and her finances in order, and repairing the relationships with those closest to her, most importantly her children. Jess considered herself lucky to have a man like Myles offer to help, but she knew this wasn't the 'be all, end all' either. There was a lot of work to be done.

Thankfully, for her, she'd just made the decision that she should start tomorrow. In the meantime, though, one last bender wouldn't hurt.

JESSICA SLIPPED INTO HER FINEST PARTY DRESS. TONIGHT WAS the Ladies Who Lunch Annual Gala. A date which no calendar need remind her of because this year it fell on her wedding anniversary. To be clearer, it was she who had planned it that way the previous year, knowing that it would be a night to remember. The Gala had always been one of her favorite annual events, and so last year, when she'd undertaken the planning she assisted in seeing that it was set for this exact day so that the day would only be that much more special. She and Spencer had won the championship dance off, seven-years running. When she thought back to the girl she'd been a year ago, she couldn't help but smile at how everything had changed. Not simply small changes, but it was as though her life were a snow globe, which someone had picked up and shook, only all of the contents were different when they landed. *Some of them were even in Africa.*

She wanted to go dancing, she had decided then and there —even if she *hadn't* been invited and even if she no longer had a dance partner. So when Jess fingered through her selection, it was an Oscar de la Renta she found fitting for the occasion. A red and black knee length dress. It wasn't what she would have chosen had she had more time, but it would do. Jess picked out a pair of earrings to pair with the dress and eyed herself in the mirror, quickly noting the way the dress once snug, now hung loosely over her body. The curves she'd once had now no longer there, she was but a skeleton of her former self, she realized as she smoothed the dress. Makeup would help and so would a drink she decided before haphazardly digging through the back of her closet in search of the bottle of vodka she had hidden there. To her dismay, in its place, she found a note that read, "I don't think so.— M"

Jess moved on to the bathroom and shuffled through the contents underneath her bathroom sink. *When had she bought all this stuff, she wondered, and why in God's name did one person need so much?* Thinking that maybe she'd forgotten where she hid the bottle, she rummaged through the contents of nearly her entire bathroom in search of the only thing she knew that would ease her anxiety. Feeling more and more desperate by the second, she tore out the innards of her vanity only to find no bottle, but yet another note. "Obviously, it is not here. Try another method of making yourself happy, instead. —M"

Damn it, she spat. Damn that man. And damn her too, for allowing herself to be babysat in this manner.

Finally, she tried her last resort. Scouring through Spencer's sock drawer, she knew the cool of the glass when she felt it with her fingertips. She reached in and gripped it tightly, pulled it out and hugged it to her chest, pleased that she'd come up fruitful this time.

Jessica untwisted the cap and took a swig, gleeful that she'd outsmarted Myles. She took another long swig and let the warmth of the alcohol ease her fears as it filled her belly. Relieved, Jess picked up a pair of her husband's socks and ran her fingers over them. She brought the bottle to her lips and took another long pull. *How had this happened to her? To her marriage? How could her husband be gay? All these years... and she'd had no idea.*

Jess took another sip and another. She promised herself only three, relented to having just four, and then gave up altogether when she'd lost count. It wasn't until the room began to sway that she replaced the cap and set the bottle aside. Unsteadily, she reached up and forcefully yanked one of her husband's shirts off the hanger. She pulled and pulled again until there were piles of them surrounding her. She studied each of them, took them in her hands, and let the memories come. It seemed each of them held a different memory . A different memory of a different time, a different place. Stripes equaled Spencer here. Solids, Spencer there. She inhaled his scent and let herself go to that familiar place. The place she so carefully avoided in the daylight, the place where she'd been loved and desired, once upon a time. It was a safe place, not like where she'd spent most of her time lately. Stuck between anyone and everyone watching her fall apart and caring all together, she replayed the Technicolor movie in her mind—of all that was had, all that was lost, and all that would *never* be again. *Her husband was gay the whole time she knew they would say, but never to her face. We all knew it — but poor Jessica, she always was so oblivious. How could she have missed it, they'd whisper. Look at all those shirts he had. How many men have that many shirts?*

She caught a glimpse of herself in the lighted floor to ceiling mirror. *All dressed up, with nowhere to go.* Jess laughed maniacally considering how far she'd fallen, just how deep she'd sunk. She considered her life now, a junkie, with no friends, a husband who was not only never coming back, but who had also squandered their money away and her life in the process.

Jess took one more look in the mirror then sunk further down and laid her forehead against the smooth, cool, hardwood flooring. *If it had been up to her, she would've chosen carpeting.* She buried her face in the shirts and let the tears fall until there were no more tears, only quiet sobs. *Look what has become of you, she thought to herself. Look at you now. Alone and empty.* It was this that played over and over in her mind until there was nothing left except darkness. She let the darkness take her and without any fight at all, she slipped willingly into the oblivion.

~

"Mommy?" she heard a small voice cry. "Mommy!"

"Mom. Wake up." A slightly older, male voice. *Jonathan.* She felt him shake her. "Mom, quit playing around. You're scaring Cate! And you're lying in throw up…" He shook her again, harder this time. Jess pictured herself responding, she heard it happening in her mind, but at the same time was somehow wise enough to know that her children weren't seeing nor hearing the same thing. She hovered in and out of consciousness, floating above herself and she saw the situation for what it was. Passed out cold while her kids were desperately trying but were unable to wake her. They were growing more and more panicked by the second and Jess herself was frantic, literally stuck inside her mind, unable to fix their problem. She heard a commotion, listened to the nanny's voice call out, then the butler's until finally, she heard Myles. Something about that voice in particular put her mind at ease.

"We tried to wake her up. She threw up," she heard Jonathan say.

"Your mom's fine." She listened to Myles assure him. "She just needs a shower, that's all. How about you guys run downstairs and put on a movie," he continued. His voice was calm but firm.

"Dean, run a cold shower, would you?"

She felt a finger slip into her mouth and remove the

vomit that was lodged inside. Jess tried to pick up her head, to assist, but found her body and her brain were no longer working in unison. Unable to move, she felt herself being lifted and carried and then wham! The shock of the cold hit. It was like a thousand tiny needles stabbing her body all at once and she was powerless to make it stop. Her limbs weighed a thousand pounds and Jess understood that she was too drunk to put up a fight. She heaved and instinctively turned sideways as she felt the liquid rise and burn as it rose up in her throat. She heaved and vomited, then vomited some more until it felt like maybe there was nothing left and the water turned warm.

Finally, she shifted and curled into a ball. She smelled of throw up and alcohol and everything pathetic, and still, the water ran. She wanted it to stop, she wanted to say as much, but the best she could do in her current drunken state was to focus on making herself as small as possible. Sometime later —time was irrelevant at this point as the room was spinning too fast—she inhaled the fresh, familiar scent of her shampoo and felt her scalp being massaged. She allowed herself to lean into the large hands as they enveloped her head. She mumbled several sentences, most of them incoherent, all but one. "This was my best dress, you know."

"You can do better," he whispered as he gently toweled her face and then to her relief, the water stopped. And even in her drunken state—as sick and pathetic and terrible as the situation was, she considered that maybe—just maybe, this was what love felt like.

∾

JESSICA SAT UP IN BED AND EYED HER CHILDREN. CATHERINE wore a look of worry while her son was obviously perturbed. She adjusted the covers and then propped herself up just a little more. Her head pounded, her throat burned, and all she wanted to do was pull the covers up over her head and sleep—but she knew she had to get through this, no matter what.

Jess patted the bed. "Climb in, you guys," she uttered, her throat dry, her head still spinning.

Catherine quickly perched herself up and splayed out on the bed while Jonathan slowly pulled a chair over. The sound grated on Jess's ears. She waited for him to sit and settle and as he did, she contemplated how quickly he'd gone from a little boy to a young man. He'd grown up so much in the past year. And she had missed so much of it. Jess took a deep breath in and let it out. She spoke slowly. "Listen, I need to talk to you guys about something, and I want you to feel free to ask me anything you want, okay?"

Catherine nodded eagerly. Jonathan simply stared and waited.

Jess inhaled, and then began carefully. "First of all, I want to talk to you guys about last night… you shouldn't have had to see me like you did. I was wrong for letting that happen. The thing is… I'm sick… but… I'm going to be going away for a few weeks in order to get better. Kind of like how I did when I was in the rehab facility. You remember?" She exhaled and felt the tears well up then spill over. "I'm really sad that I have to go… but I know I need to get well, especially for the two of you. I want you to know that I love the both of you more than anything. More than *anything* in the whole wide world. And I am sorry, *so* sorry for what I put you through over the past few months. Even if you don't understand it all right now, you will someday, and I hope you know that you should never have had to see me that sick." She paused to wipe the tears, which were running down her neck. "I know I scared you and I'm so very sorry, for all of it—"

"Drunk," Jonathan interrupted. "You mean you were drunk."

Jess nodded. "Yes, well, that too."

"What does drunk mean, Mommy?" Catherine asked her tone upbeat.

"It means I drank too much, sweetie. You know how when your dad and I tell you not to eat too much candy or it'll make you sick? Well, it's sort of like that." She eyed her son. "Only worse. Anyway, Grammy is going to come and stay with the two of you while I go and get better…"

Her daughter's face dropped. "But I don't want you to leave again."

Jess wrapped her daughter in her arms and met her son's gaze. "I don't want to leave again either, but this is something I have to do. Otherwise, I will just get sicker. And you guys —" she squeezed and then continued, "deserve so much better."

Jonathan shifted. "When is Dad coming home?"

She sighed and considered his question. "I don't know, sweetie. I wish I had a better answer for you, but he has business to attend to there."

He shook his head and stared toward the window. "Sure he does," Jonathan finally said before standing and walking to her. He handed her the notebook he'd been holding. "I wrote some stories… you know, the way we always used to do together… and I wanted you to read through them. I think they'll help you get better. "

Jess swallowed hard and took the notebook from her son's hands. "Of course they will."

Catherine lifted her head and glared at her brother. "Jonathan wrote about you, Mommy. He spends all his time now on his stories and never plays with me anymore. He says he wants to be a writer someday, that's why."

Jess looked over at her son. "I think he already is."

She shifted and cradled Catherine's head. "I am going to miss you two so much, but I hear that you can come and visit me in a few weeks and I can't wait until then." Jess bit her lip, grasping for words, afraid she might lose it and give herself away at any time. "Kit Cat, will you draw me some pictures and have Dean mail them? Jonathan, I'd really love it if you'd send a story or two to keep me company after I get through these."

Catherine reared up, her eyes all lit up. "I have the perfect idea! You need sparkles, Mommy!"

Jess kissed her daughter and watched as she darted out of the room with Jonathan following close behind. She turned over, knowing that she'd have to get up and dress. She and Myles were scheduled to leave in a few hours. But, for now, she just wanted to snuggle up, cry, and read the stories her son had created for her.

≈

CHAPTER SIXTEEN

Jessica opened the notebook her son had given her and closed it again. *Could she really do this?* She buckled her seatbelt and watched in the passenger side mirror as Myles loaded her things into the back of her SUV. Still feeling terrible, she hadn't thought to ask where they were going. And a part of her wasn't even sure she cared. Mostly, she just wanted to get this over with.

Myles opened the driver side door and climbed in pausing to look at her before starting the car. He seemed to read her mind. "I'm guessing you want to know where we're headed."

Jess shrugged. Not only did she still feel terrible, but she'd cried herself to sleep and then woke up from the nap only further drained and unsure of what year she was in. Out of it and disappointed she was in this situation to begin with, she was numb.

He studied her face. "Addison said to take you to the beach house. She thought it would be a good place to get away for a while, she said that you love it there."

She inhaled. *The beach house... She and Addison had spent*

most of their summers there together in college. And she was right. It was a place filled to the brim with good memories. "Let's hope I still love it there when this is all said and done."

Myles smirked. "Ah… there's that happy go lucky, positive girl I know so well. I knew she was in there somewhere. Well, for what it's worth, I think the ocean will do you some good…"

Jess stared out the window and watched as her house and everything that mattered to her faded from view. "If you say so." She finally replied before opening the notebook once again and began to read, deciding that she was in no mood for conversation.

HELLO,

My name is Jonathan Sawyer Clemens and I am eleven years, nine months, twenty-three days and seven hours old at the time of this writing. This is the story of my life. I hope you will enjoy it.

JSC

SHE PAUSED AND SMILED TO HERSELF AND CONTINUED ON. That boy of hers, he was something.

TODAY IS THE LAST DAY OF SIXTH GRADE. I GUESS I SHOULD BE happy about this because, you know, it's summer and all, but I'm not. You see, I'm growing up and this means I'm not a kid anymore. I'm moving into the future and I can't honestly tell you I like where this is headed. I think I saw a movie about this once. Also, my parents are getting divorced.

But only one of them knows it.

JSC

. . .

JESS READ AND REREAD WHAT HER SON HAD WRITTEN ON THE page. She closed the notebook, stared out the window, and pondered the timing of his entry. *Four months before the accident.* She had no idea that Jonathan was aware of what was happening with her marriage, and she wondered how this was even possible when she herself had completely missed it.

"Whatcha reading?" Myles asked, interrupting her thoughts.

Jess didn't respond.

"Okay... then."

Jess fingered the edge of the notebook, afraid to open it, afraid not to.

Myles stared straight ahead. "I have something I want to share with you if you're in the mood to hear it..."

Jess sighed but didn't answer.

He continued anyway. "So, I've been trying to find my ex-wife for a while now... and I think I might have found her."

Jess turned to him then, her tone stern. "What do you mean?"

Myles gripped the wheel tighter and then relaxed, but only a little. "Ever since Hailey died... there have been things I've wanted to say to her... things I *needed* to say..."

Jessica narrowed her brow. "Such as?"

He glanced her way, then shrugged, and focused back on the road. "Just stuff..."

She straightened in her seat and spoke slowly, her tone sharp. "Well, that's great. I hope me and my sobriety, or lack thereof, isn't holding you back."

Myles frowned. "You're not. Actually—"

Jess cut him off mid-sentence. "I guess you should ask yourself why she's running... why she's been so clever at hiding. You know... I'm not sure if you've considered this or not, but some people just don't want to be found."

"And you think I haven't given this some thought?"

She glared at him. "I don't know. Have you?"

Myles changed the subject and went straight for the jugular. "Say, about that old man of yours, I gathered that he's shaking you down for money… and I'm curious what you are going to do about it?"

Jess shifted in her seat and put as much distance as she could between the two of them before finally answering. "He needs it."

"And what about *you*? Do you need it?"

She deadpanned. "You don't think I can do this, do you?"

Myles watched her from the corner of his eye. "The question is… do *you* think you can?"

Jess watched the blur of the trees as they flashed by. She stared up at the cloudy sky and wished it would open up and swallow her whole. She wanted nothing more than to be anywhere other than where she was, in this car, headed toward the unknown. "I just think we should talk about what is really being said here, that's all."

"Fine. How about this… maybe, just maybe, everything isn't about *you*. And anyway, what I think about you is irrelevant."

"So you don't care one way or the other? Is that what you're saying?"

"I'm saying that I have my own stuff to deal with."

"How wonderful for you."

Myles stepped on the gas and picked up speed. "What are you afraid of, Jessica?"

She studied the speedometer and watched the needle creep upward. "Everything."

Myles swallowed. "Aside from *everything*. Dig a little deeper…"

She squeezed her eyes shut and massaged her temples

before taking a deep breath in and letting it out. "You're going too fast."

"Then ask me to slow down."

"Seriously? Slow down."

He let off the gas. "See, it's pretty simple… asking for what you want. Isn't it?"

Jessica felt the fear rise up in her throat and swallowed it back down. "Fine." She swallowed. "You want to know what I'm afraid of… I'll tell you… I'm afraid that once I'm sober that you'll bail. That I won't be the crazy, fun, Jessica, who needs managing anymore."

Myles did a double take. "First off, you're not as fun as you think you are. Secondly, can you control whether I bail or not? Can *you* control whether or not *I* like you?"

Jess shook her head, clearly over this conversation. "I don't know."

"Of course, you do." He pressed.

She sighed and relented. "No. I guess not…"

"Then let it go."

"I'm trying," she replied before removing the elastic bands from her wrist. She swept her hair up into a bun and wrapped it on top of her head. "I'm trying."

Myles eyed her for a second and then looked back at the road. *God, she was beautiful.* "Try harder."

"Do you want to know what I really think? I think this whole non-attachment thing you've got going is bullshit."

He raised one brow. "Oh?"

"Yeah, complete and total fucking bullshit…"

"You're not angry at all, are you?" He smirked.

"You know what, Myles?"

"What?"

"You like to think that you're enlightened or smarter than the rest of us because you're so open… because you can move through life without any fears—without being attached to anyone or anything... but you know what I think?"

"Tell me." *He liked her angry.*

"I think pretending that you don't care, that you're *so* open, is also a way of remaining closed."

Myles gripped the wheel tighter, but he didn't respond. Instead, he let the seed Jess had just planted within him begin to germinate.

JESS RE-OPENED THE NOTEBOOK AND REMOVED HER sunglasses. She reached back and grabbed her sweater from the back seat and wrapped it around her. *Just three more hours and she would be able to get out of this car and away from this man.* In the meantime, she had some reading to do.

HELLO,

It's me again. Today was a rough day. A boy on the playground has been bothering Kit Cat and today he hit her. Kit Cat is scared to go to school and when I tried to talk to my mom about it, she just stared into space and nodded. I don't think she heard anything I said. In fact, I know she didn't because when I threw a few crazy details in the mix, like Catherine and I running away, she didn't bat an eye. She just nodded and said uh-huh. I think something is wrong with her. I mean I know about the accident and all. But she seems different. As though maybe aliens invaded her brain and she's not even our mom anymore. Maybe it's just the shell of her body but a different operation system altogether. That's the only explanation I can come up with.

My dad said that this happens sometimes after car accidents and that it takes a while for a person to get back to their old selves. And maybe he's right.

But I prefer the alien version of the story.

JSC

HELLO,

I turned in the above writing to Mrs. Paulson as a part of our daily journal exercise. I thought that she might help Kit Cat and find out about this asshole kid bothering her, but she didn't. Anyway, I don't think I'll do that again though because she just agreed with my dad and said these things take time. And then she was extra nice and told me I didn't have to worry about my home- work for the rest of the week because I had "so much going on." What that really meant was that she felt sorry for me. Adults do that all the time. Instead of saying what you want them to say, they offer up pity instead. I don't want anyone feeling sorry for me. That's the last thing I need. Because boys like Adam Lancaster, who bother little girls, feed off pity, and then they use it to their advantage.

Sometimes, I think I'm two different people. There is the one teachers see. And the one who arranges bullies even bigger than the shithead who is messing with my sister to put the Adam Lancaster's of the world in their place.

I tried to talk to my dad about this today... mostly because I needed to know the legal implications of arranging such a thing, and I knew he would know... but as usual, his phone rang and he pulled the car over and stepped out to take the call because "this is important."

Maybe this is why my mom stopped trying.

JSC

HI,

I decided to say hi instead of hello today. I'm not sure why, and maybe this sounds weird, but I feel like we are getting to know one another and maybe hello is a little too formal. It's kind of like this girl at school named Sophie who I kind of sort of like. Every day I saw her, but never said anything. Whenever she looked my way, I just looked away. And then one day, I said hello and she said hello. And it went on and on like this for a while until 'hellos' were no longer needed, and we just started talking without all of the formalities. Sometimes, it's nice to get right down to it. And I can do that with her, which I like. It's nice to have a friend. Sophie's parents are divorced, and I always want to tell her she's not alone even though she doesn't seem to feel sad about it.

Anyway, I don't want to put too much pressure on you as a reader or anything, but it feels like maybe you are starting to understand where I am coming from. Or maybe I am starting to understand myself. This is one reason I began writing in this journal. My mom gave it to me back in the old days when I had no use for it. When she was herself. And, anyway, now everything is different, and I wanted to write about stuff that I didn't want my teachers to see. Because, you know, there's the pity thing. And it's kind of embarrassing to share your thoughts with everyone. Because sometimes they'll use those thoughts against you. But that is a story for another time. For now, this is just for me and I guess for you, too. Even though I don't know who you are.

But then again, I guess you don't really know me either.

JSC

JESS CLOSED THE NOTEBOOK. "MYLES…"

He looked her way and waited.

"Did the doctor say what the quickest way to detox was? Basically, what I mean is how long is this going to take?"

He studied her face. "The first week or two is pretty rough I hear… and I'm not sure this is something you should rush." He looked back at the road before continuing. "No worries, though. The doc will be seeing you a little later today and you can ask him yourself."

Jess exhaled. "Good. Because I really, really need to get back home."

CHAPTER SEVENTEEN

J ess and Myles arrived at the beach cottage shortly
before sunset. To Jessica, it hadn't changed much even
though she considered it had been more than a year
since she'd been there. Despite the fact she had zero energy, a
part of her wanted to run for the water, to let all of the heavi-
ness go, to swim in the ocean, feelings which driving up to
the cottage had evoked since she was a kid. But having not
had any of her medication other than alcohol within the past
twelve hours, and with her son's words settling in her bones,
she found herself feeling rather terrible and wishing that
they'd picked some other place to take her.

As Myles unloaded their things and took them inside, Jess
walked the length of the front of the old blue cottage. The
small, secluded compound had been in her family for three
generations and was now hers given that the rest of them
had deemed it too small and too much work, and thus, had
purchased their own newer, updated, and more expansive
versions of the place. But Jess had always appreciated the
charm and the quaintness of the old house. With its shut-
tered windows, wrap around porch, and stone fireplaces, she

always thought it belonged somewhere on Nantucket instead of the shores of the Texas Coast.

She ran her hands along the banister, then took a seat on the porch swing and settled in. *This is where she would get better. This is where she would find herself again.* She inhaled deeply and breathed in the salt and the sand and the cool early summer breeze coming off the water. She sat that way, in the stillness, for a long while until Myles interrupted her reverie by suggesting that they take a walk down to the water.

Though all she really felt like doing was to sit, Jess stood and followed. Myles was technically a guest and her mother had always told her not to be rude to guests. She pondered all of the things her mother had taught her over the years and wondered how many of them still served her and yet, as she caught his eye, she knew she had to go. Myles smiled at her then as though he could see right through her, reading and deciphering each and every thought she had. He waited for her to catch up and he took her hand and slid it into his. They walked in silence for some time before he spoke. "This place is beautiful. And I just want you to know that I'm happy to be here. Not because you're paying me, which is something we need to discuss, actually. But for now, I want you to know that I would do this for free." He grinned. "I like you that much."

Jess sighed. "Then why ruin it by bringing up your ex-wife in the car?"

Myles stopped abruptly and sat down in the sand, carefully pulling Jess down beside him. He studied her face and spoke slowly. "I'm not sure why that bothered you so much… but if you're willing to tell me, I'm willing to listen."

She wanted to be obtuse but couldn't help but notice the gentle way his eyes searched hers as he spoke, so she relented instead and relaxed into the conversation before letting it all spill out. "I don't know... I guess it's just that you really haven't told me much about yourself... other than not to ask any questions... and everything in my own life is so mixed up right now... that you seem to be the only constant... and then you go and dump that on me without warning. I just wasn't expecting it... that's all."

"You're right. And I'm sorry. It's been a very long time since I've shown any sort of real emotion to anyone, and I guess I'm still a little rusty about how it all works..."

Jess looked out over the water, picked up a handful of sand, and let it fall through her fingers. "I really feel like shit."

Myles cleared his throat. "It's going to be this way for a little while, but it'll get better."

"I know. I guess I just hadn't expected to feel so raw. Without the drugs, I mean. It's as though all of my armor has been stripped away and here I am."

He smiled. "Yeah. That's exactly what it's like."

Jess turned to look at him, her brow narrowed. "What do you mean?"

"I don't know what I mean... life, love maybe... it can be that way. You don't get a choice whether or not you want to hide from it. Eventually, it just catches up with you."

She laughed. "I don't know... love is a whole lot scarier, I think. It's ironic, you know... falling in love is so easy. But it's the falling out of it that sucks. As with other things, I guess falling usually doesn't hurt, but the landing sure as hell does."

He took a deep breath. "What I meant was that being with you... that's what it feels like. A little raw, but familiar too. I don't know why I'm saying this other than I think you should know... Being with you... it's like... I can breathe again—only it hurts a little and yet, at the same time, I can't suck in enough air to keep me satisfied."

Jess laughed. "Funny. That's what getting high feels like.

And then you just need more and more to do the same job. It's never enough."

Myles shifted his gaze toward the tide coming in. "No, I suppose it's not."

Jess watched the waves out in the distance. "I guess we all get addicted to something that takes the pain away." She looked over at Myles then stood and walked toward the ocean.

After a moment or so, Myles stood, brushed himself off, and followed her lead. He watched as she walked out into the water, first dipping a toe in and then both feet. "So, what was it you wanted to tell me about your ex-wife?" she asked, her tone flat.

He kicked off his flip-flops, picked them up, and tossed them away from the shore. "I wanted to tell you that maybe you're right. Maybe she doesn't want to be found…"

Jess waited for him to turn so she could see his face… "I don't know… I guess you need to ask yourself why finding her is so important. I mean… I went all the way to Africa chasing a dream and look where it got me…"

Myles inhaled, then nonchalantly reached down and brushed her hair out of her face. "It got you here, didn't it?"

Jess searched his eyes. *She could get lost in them if she let herself. But that was the thing… she couldn't. It was too dangerous of a game to play.*

Myles confirmed her thoughts as he spoke. "I don't know… I've sort of always thought that if I could just speak to her that maybe things would be different. That we could work it out. I get that… I mean… I know that no conversation will take away losing our little girl, but I would be lying if I didn't say just a small part of me believed we could create what we had again. And that perhaps, if I just tried harder, that it would all be different the next time."

"Is that what you really want? To work it out?"

"I don't know... Maybe I just want closure."

"How did Hailey die, Myles?"

Hearing her name caused him to visibly flinch. He rubbed his hand over his face and waited a while before he finally spoke. "She got sick. At first, Leslie…" He paused and sighed. "Leslie was my wife."

Jess nodded and kept her eyes on his, silently urging him to go on.

"At first, she thought it was no big deal… you know, just normal kid stuff. Hailey was only two so she seemed to constantly be picking up a cold here or there… and Leslie thought it was just another virus, like all the others. Leslie was sure if she took her to the doctor, it would be like all the other times where they just sent her home to wait it out. So, this time she didn't go. And even as Hailey's fever climbed higher and higher, she told herself it was nothing, until finally, Hailey seemed to have some sort of seizure, and so Leslie rushed her in. But, by then it was too late, she was too sick… she had meningitis all along it turned out, and she never woke up again… Leslie blamed herself and in doing so, blamed me for not being there."

Jessica squeezed his hand. "I'm so sorry."

Myles exhaled slowly. "Me, too. But she was right. I should've been there."

Jess swallowed. "As a mother, and clearly even as a shitty one these days, I understand where you're coming from, but logically—you have to know, Myles, that even if you had been there, the outcome would have likely been the same. Sometimes these things happen and there's not a lot we can do to stop them… I know that doesn't make it easier—but it's the truth. And I know that no matter what I say or what anyone else says, it won't change things for you. But if it would, I would paint your past with the truth so that you could see yourself as I see you. Brave, and kind, and caring, and most importantly, someone without so much doubt. "

Myles checked his watch. "That's sweet. But we both know you're not in your right mind, anyway," he said, playfully shoving her shoulder before he placed a hand on each one and steadied her. "We need to get you back to the house. The doc will be here in a half hour…"

Jess nodded, then reached up and took his chin between her fingers. She wanted to kiss him, but she held back and filled the empty space with words instead. "Thank you for sharing that with me. It really means a lot. You've always been a good friend to me and I appreciate that." She took a deep breath then looked away. "And I'm sorry for shutting you down earlier. I shouldn't have done that."

Myles slowly took a step back and turned toward the house. "Let's go," he called over his shoulder. "There's still plenty of time for you to feel like shit about it."

Jessica watched him go as she dug her toes further into the wet sand and squeezed them, watching as the muddy water poured over her feet and enveloped them. She let him get a ways ahead before she allowed herself to smile—just a little. All along she'd let him think he was breaking her, but maybe, just maybe, they'd actually been breaking each other.

AFTER THEY HAD ARRIVED BACK AT THE COTTAGE, JESS TOLD Myles that she was going to retreat to her room to call the kids. Which she eventually did, but first, she dialed her best friend.

The two of them exchanged brief pleasantries and then Jess got right down to it.

"Addison… listen, I need your help… something is going on here and I can't put my finger on it."

"If you need booze or drugs, I can't help you."

Jess lowered her tone. "No, it's not that. I think I might have feelings for Myles. I don't understand. One second I hate him, and the next, I can't get enough."

Addison laughed. "Yeah, that sounds about right. That's what you call love, Jess."

"Ha. Ha. No, seriously though, I've been fighting this… whatever it is… and I'm not sure that I can or even *want* to anymore."

"Then don't."

"But… I don't know what to do…"

"Just keep doing what you're doing… it's obviously working."

Jess let out a long sigh. "Addie… I don't think you understand. I don't think it's supposed to be this way. I literally want to choke him half of the time."

"That's called chemistry, Jess. Just go with it."

"Are we even in the same conversation here?"

Addison cleared her throat and spoke slowly and deliberately. "Look… I know you're scared and I know you're fighting whatever is going on here… but first and foremost, you need to get sober… and then, I promise you… things will look a little more clear. Just ease your way into it. Feel what you need to feel and quit fighting it."

"So you're saying I should just give in. That's easy for you to say…"

"No, Jess. That's love. It's not easy. And there are *no* rules. It's never as clear cut or as clean as we want it to be…"

Jess laughed. "Oh, good, now we're getting somewhere."

"So you love him then? You're admitting that you're ready to wave the white flag now?"

She thought for a moment. "I'm not sure I even know what love is…"

Addison exhaled. "Sure you do. It's caring enough that

you *want* to stick around long enough to choke them. Otherwise, you would've let him go by now. It's the need to get it right. And not wanting to do it any other way."

Jess bit her lip. "Touché."

~

JUST AS MYLES HAD SAID, THE DOCTOR ARRIVED SHORTLY before eight p.m. A plump, balding man, with large, circular rimmed glasses. He introduced himself in a gruff, tired voice as Dr. Martin.

"Too many junkies today?" Jess asked sarcastically.

The man didn't answer. Instead, he began by taking her vitals, then jotted down a few notes and asked Jess a myriad of questions about how she was feeling, which drugs were prescribed to her, and which she'd been using and at what dosage. He quizzed her on the last time she'd medicated and the last time she'd abused alcohol.

Jess told the truth about the drugs and the alcohol, but as far as how she felt, she simply said that it felt like she had a mild flu and left it at that. What she wanted to say was that her muscles ached just barely less than her heart did, and that she felt clammy and in love, too full and insatiable, all at once. She wanted to tell him that her eyes burned and they wouldn't stop running, and yet, she didn't want to close them —because it was too scary a place in the dark.

But instead, she simply nodded as the doctor advised her that she was experiencing moderate withdrawal symptoms and that they would only become more extreme from this point forward. He suggested using a medication called Naltrexone that would both speed up and minimize the detoxification process. He explained that the medication worked by attaching to one's endorphin or opiate receptors, completely blocking them, meaning that if one were to use any sort of opiate—including Jess's go-to favorites Oxycontin and Dilaudid while they are on Naltrexone, they would feel no effect because all of their receptors would be completely blocked. He explained that while Naltrexone was on board, it would be virtually impossible to relapse and that it would also help significantly with cravings that were likely to occur after detox. He informed her that there were other medications they could use as well, and he began to explain those in some detail as Jess sat quietly and focused her attention out the window.

She halfway listened as Myles drilled the physician about the pros and cons of each method before she finally decided that she'd had enough. She stood and interrupted, looking from the doctor to Myles and back again. "Is there anything else you need from me?"

Myles eyed her impatiently, his head cocked to the side. "*Why?* Have you decided on a method of treatment? Because if so, I think the two of us should discuss it first."

Jess put her hand on her hip. "Well, if either one of you would have consulted me, I could've saved you both a lot of time and a lot of going back and forth."

Both men stared at her.

"I'm going to do this cold turkey."

Dr. Martin stared down at the floor before meeting her eye again. "That really isn't advisable. Detoxing off of opiates is no walk in the park."

"Jessica," Myles pleaded his voice low.

"Look, I said I'm going cold turkey, and I've made my mind up! Maybe you don't agree… but here's the thing, Dr. Martin, I *want* to know what it feels like. I *want* to understand the feelings… I've avoided feeling for a long time now, maybe my whole life. I want to feel all of them, particularly the pain, and I want to know what it feels like to know the range of them. I want to understand that it's not *that* bad—

that I can handle it. Because the thing is... if I can't... if I can't learn to deal... then this was all for nothing, and I'll just end up using again."

Dr. Martin adjusted his glasses. He removed them and wiped them down and put them back on his face. "All right, then I guess this is settled." He stood and eyed the two of them, his expression stern. "But you have my number if you change your mind. Please call me, anytime."

Myles showed the doctor out and Jess headed straight for bed. *He was angry with her, she knew.*

She put on one of Spencer's old t-shirts and crawled into the big oversized bed. Feeling too bad to sleep, she picked up the notebook and read for a bit, then took a break to hide underneath the covers, curl up in a ball, gripping her head, and waiting out the pain.

When she found it was bearable again, she pulled the covers back and read a little more. Sometime later, Myles came in and climbed in bed. "Do you want some company?" he whispered. Jess nodded and felt him scoot in behind her, gently wrapping his arms around her.

"I'm really, really proud of you," he assured her quietly. And somewhere between the warmth of his arms, the pain, and the words she'd just read, she found the strength that kept her from crawling out of that bed and out of her own skin. As the hours went by, it was taking everything she had not to beg Myles to pick up the phone and call that doctor back and tell him to fix the problem—all of the problems— which she'd created.

∽

Hi,

Tonight has not been a good night. I can't sleep so I thought I would write to you instead. I guess, in a way, it helps me not feel so alone. Like maybe, you're out there somewhere thinking of me, too.

Anyway, about my night... to start from the beginning, most nights ever since the accident, Kit Cat cries for Mom at bedtime. She's only seven so I get it. It's tough for a seven-year-old when your mom's not around and your dad hardly ever comes home from work. So, at bedtime, I go in and I rub her back to help her fall asleep, because she only wants Mom, and if she can't have Mom (because she's in the hospital), then I'm the next best thing. Some nights though, I'm so tired that I end up falling asleep too, and then I don't sleep well because I wind up all scrunched up in Cat's little girly bed.

Tonight, Kit Cat (I have to stop calling her this ASAP, I'm too old for it now, I know, but she likes it so I try to make her happy anyhow)—tonight she woke up screaming and crying that her legs were hurting. So, I tried to calm her down and I rubbed her back but nothing was helping and she just kept crying. First, I went to find Serena (she's our Nanny even though I'm too old for a Nanny too, but I guess my mom thinks otherwise), but Serena doesn't like to be woken up she says, so she just yells at me to go back to bed and says that Catherine will be fine, even though she hasn't been the one listening to her cry for the past twenty minutes, and even though I know that she won't be fine. What she needs right now is Mom. But Mom isn't here. Obviously.

So, I go in search of the next best thing I can find that isn't Mom and clearly isn't Serena—someone, anyone to make the crying stop, but when I open the door to my parents' bedroom to ask my dad to come and help Cat, I find him standing naked in front of his computer.

And trust me... you DO NOT want to know what he was doing or what I saw on the screen.

Why anyone would want to look at that, I have no idea.

Grown up's are so strange.

I think I should tell my mom...

. . .

JSC

H*I*,

Thankfully, today wasn't so bad. We went to see my mom in the hospital. Mom's friend, Addison and her husband, William picked us up and took us there even though Dad said we couldn't go.

I like them—Addison and William, that is. They seem so normal, unlike my family with their weird late night habits and all. Sometimes, I dream about what it would be like to be their kid. But I know that would make my mom sad so I usually catch myself. No use wanting what you can't have, as my dad likes to say.

Speaking of my dad, I wanted to tell my mom about him and that man on the computer screen but her friends were there—and I didn't think it was appropriate to say in front of them, so I went for Plan B and gave her the note I'd written it in—just in case I chickened out.

Which I totally did.

JSC

H*I*,

I've learned a lot since I last wrote to you...

So, I decided to tell my friend Sophie (you remember I wrote about her before, she's the one whose parents are divorced) about my dad and what I saw him doing. Since my mom never said anything, she's in a lot of pain with the surgery she had and all, I probably shouldn't have made it worse I realized. But she never mentioned it. It was probably embarrassing for her, too.

I was really worried because I was afraid that my dad would say something weird—that he might try to talk to me about it. But he never did. Grown-ups are so good at pretending things never happened, even though we all know that they did. I hope I'm not like that when I grow up.

Anyway, sorry I keep getting off track, there's a lot going on these days... but back to Sophie. So, yeah, I told Sophie what happened. And you know what Sophie said? She said my dad is probably gay. Sophie knows about a lot of things, which surprises me. Sometimes I have to use Google just to bring myself up to speed, which I like because I've never met anyone smarter than Sophie. Once I asked her where she got her information from because I thought maybe it might be Google, too. And sometimes even Google is wrong. She says she's an old soul mostly because her parents are open and they taught her not to judge others. But also, because she's lived other lives and has experienced many things. I think this is why I like her so much. Being with Sophie is never boring.

But the things is, I knew what gay meant and there is no way that my dad could be gay—so I told her that she was crazy (which doesn't mean not smart, it just means wrong) and now she won't talk to me.

Then, because I wanted to prove her wrong, I went on my dad's computer and I looked at his search history just so I could tell her that what I saw with the men was a mistake. But I actually found out that Sophie isn't crazy. I also found out that Dad spends a lot of money on what Google informed me was internet porn, which happens to be so gross that I couldn't even look at it.

Dad always says to Mom that if you don't want the worms, you shouldn't have opened the can and he was right.

This, I'm sure mom would want to know.

But now, not only is Sophie NOT crazy, but she's not talking to me either.

And I have way more problems than I had before I opened my big mouth.

JSC

. . .

JESS STRUGGLED, FADING IN AND OUT. SHE WAS AWAKE, BUT IT was so dark that she had no idea what time it was, how long she'd been there, or even what day it was. She had no perception of time at all. She merely tossed and turned while her head pounded and her body ached. She slept restlessly, if you could call what she was doing sleep at all, and this time, she awoke tangled in soaked wet sheets, the sweat dripping off her.

The pain was too much to bear, but all Jess could focus on were the words she'd read screaming inside her head. They played over and over, taunting her, reminding her of all that she'd missed and the myriad of ways in which she'd gone wrong. Hoping for relief, she reached for Myles only to find his side of the bed empty. And in that moment, realized that she was truly all alone. She wanted to get up, to run, and to scream, to tell them it was all a trap—that she wanted out of this. That she would do anything to make it stop. But there was no one there to listen. Just her and pain and the prison of her own mind, which held her captive. She was stuck there with only the bitter taste of regret to keep her company.

CHAPTER EIGHTEEN

J ess spent the first five days at the beach cottage in complete and utter hell. In the end, cold turkey was modified just a bit when she finally agreed to let Myles give her Zofran for the vomiting, Imodium for the diarrhea, and Tylenol for the aches.

When Jess wasn't vomiting or sitting on the toilet, or falling in and out of restless—not quite sleep, she let Myles immerse her in the jetted Jacuzzi tub to ease the pain of it all and take her mind off things. There were so many times during those five days she wanted to give up, to throw in the towel. There were even a few times she welcomed death, anything to make her feel relief from the misery that engulfed her. Anything to make her feel better. But she hung on, knowing there was only one way to get back home where she was desperately needed.

During the worst of it, she clearly remembered Myles telling her repeatedly that she was going to be fine, she would get through this, and that the only way out—was through. There were times where the process reminded her of being in labor, only this time, with no epidural and no baby at the end.

In any case, Myles was an excellent caretaker. He made sure the doctor was there every day, and he had done a ton of research on the different vitamins she should take to help her body through the process, and had even come up with his own concoction. He spoon-fed, or more honestly, force fed her Jell-O and saw to it that the saline solution the doctor was giving her via IV was changed out at the appropriate times. He gave her reports of the children's day and conversed with Addison and her mother daily. Jess found it both easy and hard to be so dependent on someone. It made her uneasy. But it also solidified their friendship in many ways. When one could see you at your worst and still stick around, well, there was something to be said for that.

Thankfully, by day six, she was feeling a little better. The nausea, vomiting, and diarrhea had subsided, and the muscle aches were less achy and the feeling that bugs were crawling all over her entire body had finally petered out. She still felt bad, but at least it was now less bad than before. The detoxification process was an awakening of sorts, she realized. She found that everything was more intense, including her anxiety. She spoke with the children for the first time on day six and assured them, especially her son, that she was getting better and that she would be home soon. But she didn't address the journal. She decided she would save that for a time when they could discuss it in person, and Jess was well aware that consulting a child psychiatrist would be in everyone's best interest.

Jess seemed down after speaking with the children so Myles suggested that she get up and go sit on the porch in the sunlight-- that it would do her some good. Jess agreed but lasted all of five minutes before the bright light was just too much.

Upon coming back inside, Jess noticed Myles had moved her set up, everything she'd had at her bedside, from the bedroom to the living room where he'd opened all of the windows. She glared at him disapprovingly. "I just want to go back to bed."

He shook his head and pointed toward the couch. "The bedroom is for sleeping only from now on. It's time to get up. I know you don't feel good, but you can't hide out in bed all day."

Jess plopped down on the sofa and curled into a ball. "I'm not hiding."

Myles retreated to the kitchen and began banging around. "So, there's something I've been meaning to tell you... back in Austin, when I got bored at night in my room, I always ended up reading some of your writing. It helped me sleep and passed the time when I couldn't," he called out, his tone a little too chipper, especially for Myles.

Jess pinched the bridge of her nose. *Good God.*

He leaned over the counter and peeked around into the living room. "It's really good. That's why I put that stipulation in the contract about you writing in order to keep me hanging around."

"My writing was supposed to be private," she fumed.

He appeared around the corner holding a kettle in one hand. "Tea?"

Jess frowned. "So you aren't even going to apologize for invading my privacy?"

"No," he said and walked back into the kitchen where there was only more shuffling and banging. When it stopped, he lowered his tone. "Anyway, I put your laptop there beside the couch. And a pen and paper, in case you prefer that."

"Wonderful."

Myles reappeared then with two mugs of tea, one in each hand. He placed one in front of Jess, sat down on the loveseat opposite her, and propped his feet up. "It appears your son has the same talent that you do."

Jess sat straight up and glared at him, all the blood suddenly rushing to her head. "Oh, my God! You read that, *too*? What the hell?"

He waved her off, though he could clearly see how angry she was by the color in her cheeks. *It had been too long since her face had any color in it.* "It's no big deal, really. You're both really very talented. It's not like it was a chore or anything."

"I don't even know what to say to that," Jess said before she laid her head against the back of the sofa and stared at the ceiling.

"I think you should finish the book. And wow. I had no idea... about your friends, I mean... I'm rarely shocked and well, you're good. *Very* good." He chuckled before continuing. "And I sort of need to know what happens next."

Jess didn't speak for a long time. It was easier to pretend she hadn't heard him.

Finally, Myles stood. "Plus, if you *must* know... it was what I read that kept me around in the beginning. I fell in love with you through your words first. I'd read something and then the next morning, I'd come around the bend and up toward the main house, and there you'd be. It was eerie, like somehow I already knew you. Then, later, when I realized you were an addict, it didn't matter so much because I knew deep down who the person inside *really* was. What she was capable of. And I can't wait to see her again. That's why I want you to write and that is *why* I put it in the contract. So that you can see yourself as I see you."

Jess swallowed. "You're mistaken. You don't actually love *me*."

Myles cocked his head to the side, feigning ignorance. "Oh?"

"You love the person I once might've been. I think my son nailed me for who I am."

Myles walked to the window and stared out. He remained quiet for a while until the right words came to mind. "We see what we want to see, Jessica."

Two days later, Jess had an idea. Her son had communicated with her through his writing and she decided that maybe it was time that she returned the gesture. First, she set up an email account in Jonathan's name. Second, she called Dean with the login and password information and instructed him to give it to him when he arrived home from school.

Then she wrote.

To: JSC@addressredacted.com
From: JessicaClemens@addressredacted.com
Subject: Let's start from the beginning...

Dear Jonathan,

I'm not sure that writing you is the best course of action to take, given the importance and the gravity of the situation. But then again, I considered that you're twelve now and maybe twelve-year-old boys don't want to discuss these things face to face with their mother, and until you give me the go ahead, I will write to you about them instead. That said, I want you to know that from this day forward, I am here for *anything* and everything you want to talk about. On occasion, I may be distracted, but if you tell me 'hey, mom, this is important,' I promise you I will drop everything just to listen to what you're saying.

I want to apologize for everything that I have put you through. I know you have had to be a very tough, grown-up child for far longer than was fair. You have taken on so much responsibility, Jonathan, and I realize I am at fault for that. I have failed you in so many ways, but if you hear anything I say, I want you to hear this: I love you and even though I have done a really poor job of showing it recently, this has nothing to do with you or who you are. I am so proud of you. You have stepped up and cared for your sister and yourself in ways that you shouldn't have had to do. And for this, I am so very sorry. I promise to spend the rest of my life making it up to you. I don't mean that in all of the ways you probably think—being that you're a twelve-year-old. There will still be times when you hate me because I am a mother and it is a part of my job to see that you are cared for and safe—even if we don't agree that those things have the same meaning. But at least, you will hate me for a different reason than you hate me for now.

And I promise to do my very best to keep in mind that you are smart, and talented, and independent, and wise beyond your years.

Lastly, when can I meet this Sophie? She sounds like such a lovely girl. And please, Jonathan, tell her that she is not crazy. This is a conversation for another time but never again tell a woman she is crazy. It never ends well. :)

Yes, your father is gay. And he is figuring out his place in the world now that he is finally free to be who he really is. And even though this means that the two of us will no longer be married, I still love him very much, and we are still your parents, together or apart. He loves you very much. I hope you know this. The thing is, son, sometimes in being who we really are, we end up letting others down. So, while I know you are let down and probably confused about this, you must see the good in your father and know this isn't a choice he made lightly, if it were one he made at all. You see, either we are truly our authentic selves or we end up hiding and cover it up with things to push the truth down. And sometimes, as in my case, those things aren't good and sometimes, as in your Dad's case, they are actually fine, but it's the lies that make them bad, not the situation itself. That's exactly why I am here and why I've let you down.

I am so sorry that I missed your first letter about your dad. You should not have had to find out this way as it was in no way appropriate for someone your age. I now see that this is why he didn't want to bring you and your sister to the hospital after the accident. He must've been so ashamed. You did the right thing by coming to me, and I will be forever sorry that I let you down. But know this... your Dad is not a bad man. What he was doing (masturbation) as I'm sure you well know by this point, is not altogether a bad thing. And I am not making light of the situation by any means, but just know that you must always, always lock the door and consider the effect your actions have on another when it comes to most things in life, particularly pornography. And you wonder where you get your directness from? :)

I realize that maybe I could or should sugarcoat this given your age, but I'm no longer willing to sugarcoat the truth, Jonathan. I can see that you are too smart and too wise for that. It's like telling you the Easter Bunny or the Tooth Fairy still exists when we both know that ship has sailed. So from here out, I intend to face things head on, directly, and with the truth—both as your mother and in life as a whole.

I promise to be open and honest with you, and hope you'll do the same with me.

Even if at first it's just through our writing.

I love you so much,
Mom

CHAPTER NINETEEN

J essica awoke in the early morning hours of her ninth day being drug and alcohol-free. Restless, anxious, and unable to fall back to sleep, she picked up her computer and began surfing the internet. When she ran out of web pages to peruse, she checked her email and found this:

To: JessicaClemens@addressredacted.com
From: JSC@addressredacted.com
Subject: RE: Let's start from the beginning…

Dear Mom,

Thank you for writing.
If we're starting from the beginning, then you should know that I do not hate you.

Love,
JSC

. . .

Jess read and reread the email three times over and tried to come up with an appropriate response before she gave up, closed the laptop, and climbed out of bed. *There was so much she wanted to say.*

Instead, she tiptoed out of her room and into the guest room where Myles was sleeping. She stood in the doorway watching the rise and fall of his chest as he slept and pleaded with herself not to go in. *This isn't healthy, a little voice within whispered.*

Jess started to turn and go when his deep voice called out to her. "Can't sleep?" he whispered.

And all it took was the lure of that deep voice and she was in. Jess stood a little straighter, walked to the edge of the bed, pulled back the covers, and climbed in. She snuggled into the warmth of him as Myles arranged his body to allow her to scoot in closer. He lifted his arm and ushered her head up onto this chest and wrapped his arms around her and smoothed her hair away from her face.

"No, to answer your question, I can't sleep," she said once settled.

"Me, either."

Jess exhaled. "I feel so raw. So uneasy. Everything just seems ten thousand times more intense... it's hard to explain..."

"Are you feeling the urge to use?"

"I'm not going to say no..." She shifted then snuggled back into his embrace. "Myles?

"Yeah..."

"Do you think it's okay to trade one addiction for another?"

"I don't know... but someone wise once told me that we all have something we use to take the pain away..."

"So then what you're saying is— that some addictions are better than others?"

Myles shifted his weight from beneath her and sat up before climbing on top of her. "No. But I would like to suggest a live experiment in order to come to a definitive hypothesis."

She chuckled. "That makes zero sense."

He rested back, on his knees, pulled her upward toward him, and lifted her shirt over her head. "These things rarely do."

Jess tilted forward and kissed him, softly, before pulling back. "Clearly."

Myles carefully slid her pajama shorts down her legs as she went for the drawstring on his. He grasped her hand, pulled it away, and gently pushed her backward on the bed. He lowered and kissed her inner thighs all the way up. "I want to take my time with you," he crooned, looking up to meet her gaze.

Jess squirmed. "Speaking of that, what exactly are we doing here?"

He grinned then lowered his head back down between her legs. He tasted her briefly, teasing her before he paused to answer. "We're taking our time..."

And if Jess hadn't been addicted to him before—she certainly couldn't help herself now.

JESS AWOKE TO MYLES PLOPPING DOWN BESIDE HER ON THE bed. "Rise and shine, sunshine. Get up... it's time to go."

Jess pulled the covers over her head. "What time is it? It looks like it's still dark outside..."

"Five."

"Oh, God," she said as she tangled herself up in the duvet and rolled over. "Then why are you waking me up?"

Myles pulled the covers back and away from her face. "Your training begins today."

She pulled them back. "I don't train."

"Oh, you train." Myles laughed.

Jess sighed and sat up halfway. "I don't have workout clothes here."

He held an outfit she vaguely recognized. "I had Dean send a few things…"

Jess rolled her eyes, took the clothes from his hand, climbed out of bed, and made her way to the bathroom. She washed her face, dressed, threw her hair up, and wandered into the kitchen to find him. She felt still half out of it. *If she could just have a drink, one drink, she would feel better. Trouble is, one was never enough—and never would be.*

Myles thrust a banana in her direction and then placed a glass of water in front of her. "How are you feeling?"

Jess pushed the banana back across the counter. "Tired."

He eyed her disapprovingly. "You have to eat. It's a non-negotiable."

"I don't have an appetite," Jess countered.

He peeled the banana and held it out to her. "It'll come back. You just have to help it out a little…"

Jess relented. She shot him a look, then took a bite, and chewed. "What's on the agenda?"

Myles grinned. "Well… I want to see what you're capable of." He looked her up and down. "You look like you used to be in pretty good shape at one time."

She deadpanned and then swallowed the mouthful of banana she'd just bitten off. "Wow. Because that's exactly what every woman wants to hear."

Myles turned and placed his glass in the sink. "That's not what I meant. But I spoke with your doctor back home, and

166

he doesn't see any reason why you can't do all the stuff you used to do… with a few simple modifications."

"Nice to know," Jess said as she swallowed the last of the banana and tossed the peel in the garbage.

"Damn it, Jessica," he raised his voice startling her. "It's time to get the fuck over yourself already," he yelled slapping his palm against the counter hard. "I've been trapped in this goddamned house for days." He rubbed his hand. "You're a little better now, you're no fucking piece of cake to live with, and if I don't get out of here, I'm afraid one of us isn't going to survive. So, if I say we're going out… we're going out!"

Jess's hand flew to her chest. She doubled over and began laughing hysterically. *Myles was throwing a tantrum. Cool, calm, collected, Myles. He'd lost his shit. And she found it hilarious.*

Myles fumed. "What is so funny?"

She shook her head unable to stop it from coming out. Her entire face had turned red. She waved him off and kept laughing. *It had been so long since she'd laughed this hard. So long.* Myles went to her, took her arms in his hands, and pulled her upright. He pinned her back against the counter with his body.

Jess eyed him defiantly and waited. Without missing a beat, he used one hand to hold her wrists in place behind her back and then used the other to slide her running shorts down. He used one foot to step on them, and with the other, he pushed them across the floor.

"So it's going to be like this, huh?" he asked as he sucked her bottom lip between his teeth and then splayed her legs open with one knee. Jess grinned and then nodded ever so slightly as she quickly freed one hand, reached down, and yanked at his shorts, but once again, unable to get the drawstring undone, she gave up, reached in, wrapped her hand around the length of him, and pulled him free.

Myles eyed his cock in her hand, shook his head and

removed her hand and held it behind her back. "Who do you think is in charge here, Mrs. Clemens?"

She rubbed her chin. "I'm not sure it matters. The end game's the same either way."

"Oh, it matters," he said, his voice low and stern, before he grabbed her by the hips and lifted her up onto the counter. He intertwined his fingers with hers behind her back and held her firmly in place. He then positioned himself and pushed into her slowly.

Her breath caught as he pulled out and then slowly thrust into her again, this time harder. Jess gasped with each thrust, each of them harder and faster than the last. Myles watched her expression change, and when he could see that she was somewhere else altogether, almost there, he filled her one last time completely and then pulled out.

Jess pulled back and searched his eyes, clearly confused. "What are you doing?"

Myles adjusted himself back into his shorts and stepped back. "Showing you that the end game's not all the same... and where your inability to take me seriously will get you."

She narrowed her brow. "That's fucked up."

"So is laughing at me when I tell you to do something."

Jess folded her arms across her chest. "So, does that count as my workout, then?" she huffed pushing herself off the counter.

He studied her face. *Damn, this one was a handful.* He shook his head, bent down, picked up her shorts, and tossed them at her.

"Hardly.

❧

OUT ON THE BEACH, JESS COLLAPSED INTO THE SAND, PANTING harder than she had in a very long time. Myles had worked her over until there was nothing left to give. Her lungs burned, her head throbbed, and her body ached. He'd promised to go easy on her the first time she threatened to quit and they'd started out walking along the shore until Myles suggested a slow jog, only he kept picking up his pace and expected Jess to follow.

Now spent, she spread out in the sand and stared at the sky, trying to catch her breath. Light had just barely begun to peek over the horizon, and as she studied the colors of the sky, Jess tried to remember how long it had been since she'd been outside at this hour.

Myles stood over her, blocking her view, possibly waiting to see if she would get back up. When she didn't, he sat down beside her. Unable to breathe very well lying down, Jess propped herself up on her elbows and stared at the expanse of the ocean. Myles opened a bottle of water, took a swig, and then thrust it in her direction. Jess eyed the bottle and then him before she eventually reluctantly took it. *Clearly, she was still pissed about the kitchen incident.*

The two of them sat in silence for some time watching as the sun rose above the water and climbed higher in the sky.

Jess inhaled a deep breath and slowly let it out, her pulse finally returning to normal. "Hey, Myles."

He turned to look at her then and raised a brow.

"Don't ever fucking do that to me again. If you aren't going to finish what you start, don't bother starting it."

Myles sucked his bottom lip between his teeth. "Fair enough. So long as you understand my point."

"Yeah. I think I got it. And there's something else... just so you know... I think this is a really bad idea."

He smiled. "How so?"

"You being in love with me and me feeling like I might be in love with you."

Myles face didn't register the surprise she'd expected. "Well, then we'll just have to let it be bad until it turns good."

"And if it doesn't?"

"Then we know."

Jess swallowed. *Then we know.*

Myles turned his attention back toward the water. "Just let it be what it is, Jessica. Stop over-thinking it."

"I'm not sure I know how to do that."

He turned back to her. "Practice."

She searched his eyes. "I am."

Myles stood, dusted himself off, and extended his hand to her. "Come on, let's go finish what I started."

A smile spread across her face as she placed her hand in his. They walked back to the house, hand in hand, and then spent the remainder of the day in bed, learning about each other. About everything bad, everything good, and all the stuff in between.

~

CHAPTER TWENTY

M yles shook Jess's shoulder. "Jessica. Jessica… Jessica!" he called through gritted teeth.

He watched as she slowly aroused, awaking with an expression that was halfway between panic and confusion.

"Your husband is in the living room."

She rubbed her eyes. "My who?"

He sighed and pulled the duvet back. "Jessica, get up."

Myles had been anxious to wake her all afternoon. He missed her when she wasn't around, and the house felt so empty when she was asleep. Even if she were quiet or reading, something about her presence filled the silence. *He was becoming too attached, he knew. He had to pull back, but the timing wasn't right. Especially, not now when she needed him the most.* She had laid down for an afternoon nap three hours ago and Myles let her sleep. He knew she still felt a lot of malaise, and most days, could barely make it through lunch before she got that sleepy look on her face, and it wasn't long after that when she'd retire to her room saying she couldn't fight sleep any longer.

Jess stood up and contemplated his expression. "Why is he here?"

Myles shrugged. "Don't ask me. He's not my husband."

She shot him a go to hell look. "What I mean is when did he get back from Africa?"

He ran his fingers through his hair and exhaled. "I don't know. But a good way to find out would be to go out there and talk to him and stop asking me questions."

She stared at him expectantly. "Are you going to wait in here?"

He shrugged again. "It's as good a place as any."

Myles stayed put allowing the two of them privacy. It wasn't so much that he wanted to listen to what was being said, but he couldn't drum out the low hum of their voices and heard just about every word.

"You look like shit."

"Thanks."

"So, you're fucking the help now? Good god, Jess, what is wrong with you?"

"Who are *you* to judge *me*? And he's not 'the help,' he's my friend."

"So you're not paying him then? Or I should say *we're* not paying him?"

"There is no *us* anymore, Spence."

"We're still married."

"Why are you here?"

"You're not returning my calls or my emails... and the help that you're fucking wouldn't put you on when I called the house phone."

Jess crossed her arms and waited.

"I need the money we discussed."

Jess shifted her weight to her other foot. "I'm not giving you the money, Spence." She sighed. "I'm sorry."

"Come on, Jess. I know you're angry, but don't toy with me."

"I'm not."

"You can't be serious. I'm your husband, the father of your children—and you're going to treat me this way."

She shrugged. "I've consulted a divorce attorney and he advised against it." *She lied though she wasn't quite sure why.*

"You're serious?" Spencer searched her face.

"I'm sorry."

"Well, tell your attorney this—I'm lawyering up, too... and I'll be expecting alimony and I want custody of the kids... oh, while you're at it, you might want to inform him of this little affair of yours so he understands it won't bode so well in the courtroom."

"You don't want custody of the kids, Spencer. This is solely about money and we both know it."

He laughed maniacally. "What difference does it make? It's not like you're with them right now anyway. The staff is raising them. And has been for some time."

"I'm trying to get sober," Jess scoffed.

"Yeah, well, that's one more thing that isn't going to go over too well in court for you, sweetheart."

Myles wanted to break his neck. But he forced himself to stay put.

"You're not going to blackmail me into giving you my money or my children, Spencer. I'm here trying my damnedest to get clean. Have I made mistakes? Sure. But you caused the accident, which was the reason for me to need the pills in the first place. And then you walked out when I needed you most. You're *not* completely blameless here, Spencer. "

"You're pathetic. Are you *actually* trying to pin the fact that you're a junkie on me?"

"I don't know why you're being so cruel. I really don't. I have forgiven you, Spence. I forgive you for the way you ended our marriage. I forgive you for the accident. I forgive you for walking out afterward. I forgive you for the way you refused to bring the children to the hospital to see me when I needed to see them most. And... for how you handled the situation with Jonathan after he caught you looking at porn. I forgive you for showing up here and making all of these outlandish threats. I *even* forgive you for squandering our money away. But there's one thing that has nagged me for some time now, a little question that's been in the back of my mind that I hadn't wanted to ask... probably because I was afraid to know the answer, but I need to know... who was on the phone that night? Who was so important that it took me nearly losing my life just so you could continue your conversation?"

"That's irrelevant." Spencer huffed.

To her credit, Jess didn't let up. "You can either tell me yourself, it's your choice or I'll track down a copy of our cell phone bill... but I need to know."

Myles heard the front door open. "You're fucking crazy, you know that?" He heard Spencer remark followed by the door slamming so hard the paintings on the walls shook. He flew into the living room to find Jess staring at the door, her mouth gaping open, and her face drained of all color. Myles preemptively closed the gap between them, knowing she was about to sink to the floor. Sure enough, he caught her mid-fall and helped her down to the floor gently.

Jess caved and began sobbing silently.

He took her in his arms and held her. "Shhh. *Good girl.* You did good...."

When the sobs finally subsided, Myles stood, untangled himself, went to the kitchen, and returned with a glass of water.

"He's going to fight me for the children. And it's all going to come out... my drug use... everything... but you know what? I don't even care about any of that. What bothers me the most, what I care about the most, is that he just might win..."

"He won't win."

"He could."

"You're right, he could. And with that attitude, Jess, you don't stand a chance. What you need to do is to strike preemptively. Have you *actually* consulted an attorney? Because if not, you need to do so... now."

She shook her head and exhaled loudly. "I need a drink... or something... an Oxy, Xanax... I don't know. Just anything."

"What you need is a long walk and a damn good attorney. You're letting him win, Jessica. Especially, if you let this crush your sobriety—which, I'm sure I don't have to remind you, is still very much in its infancy."

"I just don't understand. This just doesn't seem like Spence—he's always been a hard-driven businessman to the core, sure... but I can't believe he would play *this* dirty... with me, with our children..."

"Desperate people do desperate things."

Jess searched his face then stared at the floor. "Tell me about it."

MYLES DID HIS BEST TO KEEP HER BUSY OVER THE NEXT several days so as to take her mind off her dissolving marital situation and the cravings of needing to use again. The afternoon Spencer showed up, Jess had a bit of a temper tantrum. After her meltdown, she retreated to the master bedroom and had one of a different kind. Upon deciding that she found nothing of herself in it or in its contents, she began tearing clothing out of drawers and closets and paintings off the walls. Myles heard the ruckus and considered her actions, leaving her to it until she emerged from the bedroom disheveled holding a pile of her husband's things. *This was getting interesting. She was so beautiful when she was angry.*

He eyed her as she marched past, his expression giving nothing away. He watched her walk out to the fire pit on the back lawn as she dumped them in. *Let's see her try to start this thing. She hasn't a clue.* She took a step back and considered her next move. Myles walked out onto the patio and took a seat. "You've never lit the fire pit before?"

She shook her head and stared at the pile of things she'd assembled.

"Have you considered donating this stuff instead?" He nodded toward the fire pit and then glared at Jess. "I mean, I understand your reasoning and all... it's just that I can see that your husband clearly has very expensive taste, and I know a whole heck of a lot of people who sure could use some of those items."

Jess cocked her head to the side. "But donating them would negate the whole point of burning them just to stick it to him."

"Either way, he's without them, Jessica."

She smiled then and her whole face lit up. "Good point. I like you."

"I'm glad. You're one of the few these days," he said, playfully mocking her.

Jess placed one hand on her hip. *God, how he wanted to give her something to smile about at that moment.* "So, who are these people you speak of that need this stuff? How would I find them?"

Myles patted the chair beside him and beckoned her over. She walked over, eyed the seat, and plopped down in his lap instead, catching him off guard. Myles had adjusted himself and her on his lap before he answered. "Well, to answer your question, there are a lot of people who could use them. Hell, half of the town I grew up in could use them. But I was specifically speaking of men serving in the military. Some of them, like me, come back to nothing. Often times, there's nothing and no one awaiting their return, and I'm sure a few things that might give them a chance at a fresh start would do them some good."

"Where's this town you speak of?"

"You're asking where I grew up?"

Jess pursed her lips and answered indirectly, being careful not to push too far.

She was good, this one. "Just a small town in East Texas. They're pretty much all the same."

"Tell me about your childhood. I don't know anything about you…"

He shifted. *Fine, he'd give just a little. He figured she'd earned it.* "There's really not a whole lot to know. My mom got knocked up just out of high school. We didn't have a lot of money, but she always did the best she could. And then she died when I was sixteen."

Jess frowned. "How did she die?"

Myles sighed. "A broken heart."

"What do you mean?" she asked, biting her lip.

"My father… or the guy who got my mom pregnant, I should say, was some businessman who was a bit older and was apparently pretty well off. He was visiting the town she lived in scouting out places to build his next hotel and went into the diner where my mom worked. She waited on him and not long after, fell in love with him. He promised her the moon and stars, and she apparently believed him. He always told her that he was getting things settled back in Houston where he was from and would send for us. In the meantime, he gave my mom money, but not so much that she didn't still have to pull doubles at the diner. And when I was around two or so, she found out the truth. That he was married with a wife and kids back in Houston. And probably, who knows how many more elsewhere. This was before the internet when it wasn't as easy to find out so much about people. Anyway, she confronted him and he cut her off. We never heard from him again…"

"Wow. Do you know his name?"

Myles nodded slowly. *Did he ever.* "Samuel Ingram."

Jess did a double take. "*The* Samuel Ingram? As in Ingram Enterprises? The hotelier?"

"That would be the one."

Her hand flew to her mouth. "Oh, my God, Myles. Do you have any idea what this means? You're entitled to a big piece of that fortune."

He shook his head. "I've never been interested in money, Jessica. It's not what makes people happy."

She sighed. "Clearly." She quickly repositioned herself on his lap and then smiled half-heartedly. "Tell me something I don't know…"

"Okay." He paused and eyed her. "My mom didn't actually die of a broken heart… she drank herself to death."

Jess inhaled sharply. *She hadn't expected that one.* "That's why you don't drink."

"That's one reason."

She swallowed, suddenly seeing things so clearly. "I see. Why did you leave the Navy?"

He cocked his head to the side. *That's enough. Game over.* "You're full of questions today, aren't you?"

"So long as you're full of answers…" She grinned.

Myles lifted her off of him and stood. *He needed to fuck her. About twenty minutes ago.* "I'm done with this game. Is there anything else you wanted to accomplish today aside from interrogation?"

She considered his question for a moment before responding. "Yeah, actually… I want to repaint the master bedroom. I didn't choose that color and to tell you the truth, I've never much liked it."

"*You* want to paint?"

She narrowed her brow. "Yeah, I've never painted a room before."

He snorted. "I figured as much. You don't strike me as the type who likes to get her hands dirty."

She glared at him ruefully. "Things change you know, people change."

"*Really?* You've never painted? *Ever?*" he asked, toying with her, feigning shock. *Of course, she hadn't.*

Jess turned to go inside and paused in the doorway. "Never."

There's something very beautiful about doing the ordinary things in life, he'd said to her..

He laughed. "Well… grab the keys because there's a first time for everything."

Myles drove Jess to the hardware store where he picked out the supplies they would need while she picked out a paint color that was more suited to her tastes called Gray Area. A fitting name they ultimately decided and that was it, the deal was sealed. And no matter how much time had gone by, whenever Jess looked at that paint on the wall, she would forever remember the feeling of standing in that store beside him on that summer day and know what it felt like to be both staring down the unknown and at the same time, to feel such hope for the future. It was both an ending and a beginning. It was everything.

~

CHAPTER TWENTY-ONE

Myles and Jessica lay there in silence on the floor of her half painted bedroom, inhaling each other, dizzy from paint fumes, and love, lost and found. They stayed like that, talking, and then made love, painted, and then made love again. The next several days went on like this, though once the painting was finished, they decided that it was time to get out of the house, each of them a little too scared at the intensity at which things were developing. To distract themselves, they paid a visit to the local aquarium, went for drives, and took long walks along the beach. It was on one of those walks Jess brought up bringing the kids down from Austin.

"I think it's time," she'd said. "I'm ready."

"Are you sure?" Myles asked.

They walked the shoreline in silence for a few paces before Jess answered. "I think so. I need to make amends with two of my most favorite people, and it just feels like now is as good as time as any." She eyed him and smiled. "No, scratch that—it feels like now is the best time."

"Then you should go for it. I'll call Dean and have him drive them up tomorrow if you want..."

She stopped and fidgeted with the hem of her shorts. "Thank you, Myles."

He studied her with a smirk upon his face, sensing there was more she wanted to say, but couldn't, or wouldn't let herself go there—yet. "It's no problem."

Jess focused on the water pooling around her feet. "I know, but still. I'm nervous. It's a big job and I'm not sure I even stand a chance..."

"I think you can do whatever you put your mind to."

"I wonder if I'm capable, that's all. I mean there's a lot to make up for when you consider all of the mistakes I've made... and obviously, there have been many..."

"They're children. They're resilient. Every parent makes mistakes, Jess. But when you know better, you do better. So, do it. It's only as hard as you make it, just my two cents. Just make sure you make it meaningful. They really only want what we all want."

She appeared confused. "And that would be?"

"I don't know... Love. Resonance. To be understood."

Jess laughed. "Yeah, so, in other words, no big deal, right?"

"Right."

"Oh, yeah, before I forget... I had Addison pick them up, so they're with her. When you talk to him, tell Dean that I'll let Addison know that he'll be picking them up."

"Smart move."

She swallowed. "I didn't want Spencer to get them until we'd had another chance to talk. I want to make sure that he has calmed down and isn't going to pull anything funny. I'm pretty sure he's all talk, but I wasn't going to take any chances..."

"Makes sense," he said before he paused and stared at their feet in the water. "I think you and I should cool it when the kids arrive." He sighed and ran his fingers through his hair. "They've been through a lot—a lot of changes, and I think it's best if what we have here doesn't add to that *or* take away from what you're trying to accomplish." He looked up at her then and smiled. "I'm sure you understand."

Jess stepped forward and pressed her body against his, and wrapped her arms around his neck. She stood on her tippy toes and kissed him before pulling back. "Smart move."

Myles threw his head back and laughed. "I'm full of 'em. Come on—" He took her hand. "Let's get back and make up for some of this time we're about to lose."

Jess placed her hand in his. "You're a good guy, Mr. Ingram."

He smiled. "You're probably one of the few people who thinks so."

She looked over at him. "You keep saying that... *but* I don't buy it."

Myles took her hand, raised it up, and twirled her around, wrapping her up into him in one of his long forgotten dance moves. "I'm glad," he'd said, leaning in, and kissing the tip of her nose before pushing her back out.

"Not bad," Jess exclaimed, surprised at his ability to direct her exactly where he wanted her to go. "I suspect you're talented in more areas than just the bedroom." She thought for a second and then added. "And the kitchen. Oh, and the bathroom..."

Myles grinned. "You ain't seen nothin' yet."

MYLES LIT A FIRE IN THE PIT WHILE JESS SAT ON THE EDGE AND watched as he made it come to life. He'd encouraged her to burn at least one of Spencer's shirts, given that had been her intention to begin with, and maybe she'd needed to do it, he'd said. *Plus*

that one is so ugly no one would want it anyway, he'd said. You always see it in movies, there's nothing like a woman scorned, he teased. But men, or most men, don't really care about clothes, he'd casually mentioned. Spencer cares, she'd retorted as she tore off the buttons, one by one, and threw them in. She held onto the shirt for a while and for reasons unknown to her, maybe instinct, she brought it up to her nose and inhaled one last time before she released it down into the flames and watched it burn.

"I think I'm going to give him the money," she finally said. "On the condition that I get full custody of the kids and a quick divorce... I just want to close this chapter of my life as smoothly as possible and if that means giving him the money in order for his cooperation, then so be it."

Myles watched the flames dance. *He wasn't surprised.* "That's a very mature position to take."

She snorted. "I don't know whether it's mature or stupid." She offered up a tight-lipped smile and then continued. "But it seems like the right thing to do for me... and especially for the kids. They've been through so much already. Seeing their parents go through a bitter divorce battle isn't something I want."

"This sobriety thing looks good on you. You know, you're a lot wiser than you give yourself credit for, Jessica."

She smiled wryly... *"You* ain't seen nothin' yet."

He poked the fire and then met her gaze. *How could he have ever not loved her?* "No, I'm sure I haven't."

THE FOLLOWING MORNING, THEY WERE AWAKENED BY A LOUD and urgent knock at the front door. Jess sat up, her expression panicked as she eyed Myles. "It's too early to be the kids, right."

He checked his watch. "Dean said around one o' clock or so."

Jess frowned. "I'll get it."

She tossed a robe over Myles's t-shirt that she had thrown on, walked to the alarm system, and punched in the code. There was more knocking followed by the doorbell. "Coming!" Jess called as she hurried to the front door. She looked out the peephole and her heart sank. *Oh, no. This couldn't mean anything good.*

Jess slowly opened the door and eyed the uniformed officers. "Mrs. Clemens?"

"Yes," she answered her voice quivering. Myles was quickly at her side.

"Can we come inside?" the female officer asked, holding up her badge. "I'm Agent Hewitt with the FBI. And this is my partner, Agent James Lewis."

Myles opened the door wider and Jess stepped aside.

She eyed the officers expectantly.

"Why don't you take a seat, Mrs. Clemens."

"How can we help you?" Myles asked his voice steady.

The female officer cocked her head and studied Myles for a moment before answering. In her black pantsuit, not a wrinkle in sight, trim with her red bob, not a nary hair out of place she looked as though she were ready to pounce. "And you are?"

He extended his hand. "Myles Ingram. I'm on Mrs. Clemens's staff."

The red head didn't blink and the male officer tipped back on his heels, and shoved his hands in his pockets. "Right," the woman finally said.

Jess took a seat. "All right. I'm sitting." She folded her arms across her chest. "What's this all about?"

The woman took a seat adjacent to Jessica. The male

officer stood at the red head's side, looking over her shoulder. *It was obvious who ran the show here, Jess thought.*

"Your husband is Spencer Clemens, is that correct?"

Jess swallowed. "He's my soon to be ex-husband, yes. Why? Is everything okay?" Her hand flew to her mouth.

"We have your husband detained, Mrs. Clemens. He's been under investigation for embezzlement for several months now. Given new information we received this week, we're also considering extortion and attempted murder charges, among others."

Jess cocked her head and narrowed her gaze. *The room was spinning.* Myles took a seat beside her. "I don't understand..."

"We have significant evidence that your husband embezzled millions in investor funds—fraudulently, obviously."

"Oh my god." Jess pinched the bridge of her nose.

"We also have reason to believe that the accident you were in earlier this year may have been planned."

Jess's eyes widened.

"Can you tell us about that, Mrs. Clemens?"

She blew out all of the air she held in her lungs. Myles stood and began to pace the length of the living room. "But *why* would he do such a thing? I don't think my husband, Spencer, *my* Spencer is capable of what you're suggesting..."

"You'd be surprised what some people are capable of, Mrs. Clemens."

"Jessica. Please, call me. Jessica."

The woman nodded and looked at her partner briefly before continuing. "Jessica. Do you know anyone by the name of David Dewitt? Is that name familiar to you?"

Jess thought for a moment and then shook her head. "No. I don't think so."

"He claims to have been your husband's lover for the past two years. And he has provided us with information, which suggests that the accident you were involved in may have been intentional. So we need you to cooperate with us and tell us everything you can about that night."

She wasn't going there. Not now. "And if I don't remember?"

The agent exhaled slowly and deliberately. "Either way, your husband looks to spend a solid portion of the rest of his life behind bars, Mrs. Clemens." She paused, corrected herself, and went on. "Jessica. And the more you cooperate with our investigation, the more we can ensure that the information our informant has provided is correct."

Jess cocked her head. "I don't know what you want me to say. This is all so ludicrous. I just can't imagine—"

"Mrs. Clemens," the woman interrupted, "my job here is to make sure that you're aware of the severity of the situation here. We have reason to believe that your husband may have purposely tried to kill you. And whether or not this information is ultimately proven true depends a lot on your level of cooperation. But aside from that, your husband stole an awful lot of money from some very hardworking folks. So, the other part of my job is to sort fact from fiction here and to help us ensure that you were not aware and thus, cannot be held responsible for your husband's actions—given that the two of you are still legally married and all of the financial implications that come *with* that. Were you aware of any insurance policies that your husband may have taken out on your behalf? Did he speak of having money troubles?"

Jess covered her face with her hands. "Um... I don't know. Oh, God. How *could* this happen? How *can* this be happening? I just don't understand..."

Myles ran his fingers through his hair and then stepped forward. "Jessica," he said. Her name came out hard, his tone serious. "That's enough for now," he commanded.

He turned to the male agent but eyed the redhead. "My boss would prefer to have her attorney present before any further discussions take place, Miss Hewitt. I'm sure you can understand the shock she's in right now, so if it's all the same to you, I think it's best we give her a little time to process this and to get in touch with her legal team."

The woman nodded and stood to face him as if she'd expected it. "Okay. Here's my card." She reached into her suit pocket. "Please contact me as soon as possible with Mrs. Clemens's attorney's information. Or have the counsel contact me themselves—that's probably best." She sized Myles up and turned away from Jess and spoke as if she were no longer in the room. "We really prefer Mrs. Clemens's cooperation in this matter. Please make that clear, would you, Mr. Ingram?"

"I will." Myles nodded. "Let me show you out," he said as he ushered the two of them toward the door. "I absolutely will," he added once more for good measure as he shut the door.

He stood at the door and stared at the back of it. He balled his fists. "If I don't kill the bastard myself first," he muttered to no one in particular.

Jess just sat staring into space, hoping that he'd say something, *anything*, to make it all better. He turned to her as though he'd read her mind. Her eyes were wide and glazed over. She was in shock, he understood. But he recognized the expression that she wore as one of understanding. Suddenly, to her, everything and nothing at all made sense.

CHAPTER TWENTY-TWO

"What am I going to do?" Jess asked into thin air, speaking perhaps to Myles, but more likely to no one in particular.

He had already picked up the phone and had begun to dial Addison. "Hey," he said abruptly. "It's Myles. I need to know how to contact Jessica's family's attorneys…"

She listened as he recanted the story of what had just taken place and watched as he jotted down a few notes on a notepad. When he was done, he tore off the piece of paper and handed it to her.

"Here. Addison said this is the guy your father always used."

Jess placed the slip of paper on the coffee table and stared at the floor. "Right. I should have thought of that…"

Myles sat down beside her and rested his hand on her thigh if for no other reason than to get her attention. "You need to give them a call, right now."

She turned to face him. "Do you think that he could have done that with the accident? I just don't know… and yet so many things are starting to make more sense."

"I don't know. Let the cops figure that one out... Your job right now is to protect yourself."

"They could take everything, Myles. I've watched enough TV in my life to know how this works..."

"Look, Jessica... worst case is it sounds like it could cost you millions... but, like I said, that's not for you to worry about right now. Call your father's attorneys," he urged, handing her the phone.

She placed the call and was immediately passed through to James Horowitz. James was the attorney her father had used for at least the past thirty years or as long as Jess could remember. Their families had vacationed together for years growing up. He was a good attorney, the best her father always said, and when he picked up, she gave him all of the information she had, and he assured her that he'd put his finest team on the case.

The children arrived on schedule, around one o'clock and suddenly, the house was teeming with people. From the chef, to the nanny, to Dean—the butler and the instant chaos of having the children there and all of the commotion seemed to help take Jess's mind off everything.

That afternoon, as she sat out on the beach watching the kids play in the water, she wondered just what she'd tell them about their father if the allegations turned out to be true. Ultimately, she realized that he would always be their dad, no matter what, and she would do her best, for them, not to tarnish that.

As Jess was pondering how she might go about telling them, Jonathan sauntered in from the water and plopped down beside her in the sand. "I'm so glad you guys are here," Jess said to him.

"Are you coming back home with us, Mom?"

She considered his question for a moment before answering. "I figured we could stay here for a while. What do you think?"

"You mean for the whole summer?"

She nodded.

"I don't know. I'd miss my friends…"

"We could have them come down."

He shrugged.

Jess eyed him. "We'll figure it out."

"I'm glad you're feeling better," he said, staring out at his sister playing in the water.

"Me too, sweetie. Me, too."

THREE DAYS LATER, JESS AND MYLES DROVE BACK TO AUSTIN for the day so that she could meet with her attorneys. She trepidly entered her lawyer's office, not exactly sure what to expect, only to find that her entire life had been laid out before her in a series of spreadsheets and financial documents and timelines on a conference room table.

Over the previous two days, Jess had given the lawyers and their staff members all of the information she had. The calls back and forth had been endless, and now it was all spread out before her like pieces of a puzzle that she wasn't sure she wanted to put together. James Horowitz had met with the FBI agents himself and had come armed with his own information.

As she entered the conference room to find out precisely what this information was, she was met by four suits sitting in a row, around a table with room for at least twenty. They all stood at once to greet her. Jess shook their hands one by one. Myles pulled out her chair. She took a seat and the suits followed.

"How's your father, dear?" James Horowitz asked, being the first to speak.

"He's fine, I hear. Mom says he still recognizes her occasionally. Actually, I haven't been to see him in a while. I need to get by there..." Jess replied unsure of why she offered up so much information and attributed it to nerves.

The older man nodded in understanding and glanced down at the documents in front of him. "Your father was a brilliant man, Jessica. I am very proud to have had the opportunity to call him a friend for so many years. It's such a shame, you know, but... the good news is that he set his family up very well. We did a seamless job at setting things up initially, from the beginning, so that your husband couldn't touch your fortune."

Jess swallowed. "Spencer had my father sign some papers about a year ago, giving him control. I remember him talking about it..."

"First off, your husband, even with those documents, was only able to access very little of your inheritance. Secondly, we can prove that your father, given the Alzheimer's diagnosis, was in no condition to sign that paperwork. This provides significant protection."

Jess exhaled. "How much was he able to get?"

"Three and a half million," a younger man answered, pointing at one of the documents on the table. "And it does appear that he squandered, or at the very least has hidden, your marital assets very well. We are still getting information in on several of the accounts."

"But my father's money and my inheritance are both intact?"

"Yes." He pointed at the spreadsheet as though she were aware of what it all meant. "Your father made some very sound decisions regarding who had access to these particular accounts."

"But this is why you need to cooperate with the FBI, Jessica," Mr. Horowitz chimed in. "Your husband is being accused of some very serious accusations and our job is to show that you were also a victim in all of this, not an accomplice. And given what you've relayed to my staff, I don't suspect that this should be too hard to prove. But defending yourself in this won't come cheap—especially if you choose not to make friends with the feds. After speaking with them, it seems they also believe you to be an innocent bystander, and let me tell you, the more you have them on your side, the better off you'll be."

Jess reached into her bag, pulled out a folder, and slid it across the table. "I've written down in detail everything I can remember about the past year... including all of the details of the accident."

One of the men reached for the folder, opened it, and began scanning the documents. He looked up at Jess, his expression pleased. "This is great. It should help a lot."

"Do you believe your husband intentionally caused the accident as his lover suggests, Mrs. Clemens?" another one of the suits quizzed.

Jess bit her lip. "I'm not sure what to believe. In the last few weeks, my entire life has suddenly become unrecognizable. I wasn't aware my husband even had a lover, among other things."

"According to this guy—" He glanced down at a paper in front of him. "A man by the name of David Dewitt—your husband believed that upon your death that he stood to inherit the entirety of your worth according to your prenup, as well as a life insurance policy valued at twenty-five million. Do you remember taking out this policy, Mrs. Clemens?"

"Yes, after our son was born. Spencer thought it would be a good idea—"

"Had you ever heard the name David Dewitt prior to today?"

"Only when the FBI mentioned it…"

"Well, he was involved in the scheme your husband used to steal from unsuspecting investors. And he's now working with the feds on a plea bargain deal provided that he helps with the investigation against your husband."

"I see."

"Do you remember your husband getting a phone call the night of the accident?"

Jess looked down at the table and nodded.

"Mr. Dewitt claims that he was instructed to call your husband's cell phone at midnight. In fact, he's given a pretty compelling testimony about what occurred that night."

She felt the knife in her back begin to twist. "I'm not sure what to say."

"How was your marriage prior to the accident, Mrs. Clemens?"

Jess motioned toward the folder. Myles had encouraged her to write it all out. *You're a writer, he'd said. Use it to your advantage. Do what you know.* "It's all in there. Everything," she uttered.

A second suit took the folder from the one firing off the questions. He studied it, flipping through the pages.

"Looks like you wrote us a novel here."

Jess smiled faintly. "Something like that." Then she stood. "Like, I said, it's all in there. Now, if you'll excuse me, I really need to get back to my children."

Myles watched her for a second before he stood himself.

"We'll be in touch, Jessica," Mr. Horowitz said slowly rising to his feet. He extended both of his hands and took her hand in his. "Try not to worry too much. I promise, we'll get this all sorted out. You just let us take care of it, will you?

And… get by there to see your father, okay? You always were his favorite subject, you know."

She swallowed hard. "I will."

"Very well." The old man smiled.

Jess let Myles pull out her chair and she walked to the door pausing just inside. "Oh. One last thing… when can I see Spencer?"

One of the suits straightened his back. "That's not advisable at this time, Mrs. Clemens."

She eyed the man, glanced down at the floor, and then met his gaze head on. "No, I don't suppose it is."

JESS, MYLES, THE CHILDREN, AND A FEW OF HER STAFF members did end up spending the remainder of the summer at the beach house. Once the press got a hold of the story, it made it nearly impossible to return home and maintain any sort of normalcy. To protect the children as much as she could, she decided they would remain there at least until school started.

When Jess returned home from her attorney's office, she sat Jonathan and Catherine down in the living room.

"Your dad is in some pretty serious trouble," she'd said matter of factly.

"What kind of trouble?" Jonathan asked immediately.

"Well, let's just say that he stole from people and is being accused of some very bad things—but the truth is that we don't have all of the facts. And even more so, he is still your father and I know that no matter what happens, he loves you both very much."

"Is he going to jail?" Catherine quizzed.

Jess braced herself. "He is in jail, sweetheart."

Jonathan stood and walked out of the room without another word.

"When is he coming home?" Cat cried.

Jess took her daughter in her arms. "I don't know, sweetie."

She always questioned herself about whether or not she told them too soon. Maybe she should have pretended he was still in Africa, at least for the summer, she considered. She'd handled so many things wrong over the past year, but this one, she was determined to be honest about. And to the extent that she could—given the circumstances, this was one she hoped to get right.

JESS KNOCKED QUIETLY AND ENTERED HER SON'S ROOM. HE was sitting on the floor, his back against his bed tossing a rubber ball at the wall.

"How's Cat?" he asked without looking up.

"She's okay, I think. Myles took her into town for ice cream..." Jess folded her arms and leaned into the door jam. She nodded toward the bed. "Can I sit?"

Jonathan shrugged nonchalantly.

Jess made her way over to the bed and sat on the end of it. "I know this is a lot to take in. And I know you're too old to be distracted by ice cream... but is there anything I can do? Do you have any questions?"

"This is so embarrassing. I'm pretty sure that Sophie will never talk to me again. Now that my dad's a criminal..."

Jess inhaled and let it out slowly. "I don't know so much about that. If this girl is anything like you wrote, she seems pretty understanding... Just don't call her crazy," she said, trying to make light of the situation.

"I hate him."

Jess lightly placed her hand on her son's shoulder. "You don't hate him, son. You're just angry, which is understandable."

"I do hate him. He has ruined our whole lives."

"Not our whole lives, Jonathan. There's still so much more than this. You know... I understand you're hurt, and you should be... but all the best people have lived through some pretty horrible experiences in their lives and come out on the other side, better for it. And the thing is, Jonathan, what your dad did doesn't say anything about who you are."

"Try telling the kids at school that." He huffed.

"Fuck the kids at school."

She'd gotten his attention then. He looked up at her. "Seriously, fuck them. If you live your life according to how everyone else measures you up, then you're set for a lifetime of disappointment. Now, don't get me wrong. I know I've done a terrible job of demonstrating this for you... but I promise to do better from now on. I promise."

"You've done okay. You're not like the other moms..."

She snorted. "That's for sure. But I tried to be for so long. Too long. But the thing is... half of them don't even know who they are. We were just the blind leading the blind. It takes guts to step out of line and be who you really are. Flaws and all."

"Why would he steal money, Mom? It's like he didn't even care about us."

"I don't know. I really don't. I wish I had all the answers for you, but the truth is I don't have any of them. And to be really honest, we may never know. Maybe you should write to him. He probably can't give you the answers either... but I do know that he does care about you. I was there the day you were born, and I saw the way his face lit up when he saw you for the first time. And no matter what he did, or what anybody says about him, for the rest of my life—*that's* the man I'll remember."

"So what you're saying is to pretend like he didn't screw us over?"

"No. What I'm saying is that ultimately he screwed himself over. And for our own sake, it might be a good idea to try to remember all of the good things about him. I'm not saying not to be angry, or sad, or hurt... but it won't change what he's done."

He sighed. "Mom?"

"Yes."

"Can I say fuck?"

She pursed her lips. "Just once. And that was your once, just then."

"Okay. Well, in that case, I want ice cream, too."

Jess laughed. "Then we better get a move on it, if we're going to catch them."

This was how they spent the rest of that summer—stuck somewhere between sadness, anger, and understanding. With just a touch of hope sprinkled in.

CHAPTER TWENTY-THREE

They returned home in late August just before school started. The press had mostly lost interest and moved on to other things—at least until the trial started that is. Jess still hadn't told the children the full extent of the charges against their father, but knew that time was running out given that school was set to start, and if she didn't tell them, someone else likely would. How she could possibly have that conversation with them, she wasn't sure, so much so that she nearly vetoed going home altogether. But it was time. And in the end, unavoidable.

Jess wanted to visit Spencer in jail even though her attorneys had advised against it. She needed to get answers and she'd planned to do so, but he'd declined each of her requests for visitation. Finally, she wrote him a letter, which she'd asked Jonathan to stick in with his and a few of Cat's drawings.

DEAR SPENCER,
   Honestly, I'm not sure where to start.

I am still in disbelief over what has taken place, and I still hold some hope that the allegations about the accident aren't true. I would have given you the money, and I thought you knew me well enough to know that, which is why none of this makes any sense. I'm not even sure how it's possible to sleep in the same bed as someone who wishes you dead and still have no idea.

But I will say this—I forgive you.

Even if I can't yet forgive myself, I forgive you. Because the truth is, you didn't get the best of me, Spencer. What you've done to our family is incomprehensible and still, the children and I will be okay in the end. You, on the other hand, will have a very long time to sit and ponder it all and all that you're missing. And my only question to you is for what?

My heart is broken for the kids and yet it is for them that I realize that I must forgive you.

Jessica

OVER THE COURSE OF THE SUMMER, THE CHILDREN HAD REALLY taken to Myles and him to them. He and Jess let their level of affection evolve slowly around the kids until they were practically the only ones still in on their bad joke.

"I know you love him," Jonathan mentioned casually over breakfast one morning as Myles walked out the door.

Jess had watched him go and turned her attention back to her son. "I don't love him," she'd countered, smiling. "But I like him an awful lot."

"Clearly," Catherine had added.

"It's okay if you do," Jonathan said. "Just don't lie about it."

She gulped her orange juice and swallowed. "All right. Geez! You two are tough."

And just like that, the cat was out of the bag.

THREE DAYS BEFORE SCHOOL WAS TO START BACK, JESS SAT Jonathan down and handed him her notebook, turned to the correct page. "I'm not sure I can say it aloud to you. I hope you'll forgive me, but I wrote it for you instead. It's the best I could do."

Hesitantly, he pulled the notebook into his lap. She watched him read it and noted how his shoulders slumped and his eyes grew wide as he scanned the pages.

"I fucking hate him. I told you I did."

Her eyes filled with tears. "I'm sorry, son. I didn't want this to be the way it was either."

"I never want to talk to him as long as I live," he said.

"I hear you. I hope you'll change your mind. But I understand… and that was your one fuck."

"Fuck him. Fuck him. Fuck him. He tried to kill you. Fuck him."

"Jonathan, stop. You're a writer. How about taking all of that frustration and anger and putting it on paper? It's helped me—"

"I just want to be alone now," he interrupted.

She waited for a moment, hoping her son would change his mind, but when he handed her the notebook and motioned toward the door, she simply nodded. Jess ran her fingers through his hair sloppily before giving in and going. *There were so many things she couldn't fix for him now no matter how hard she tried.* Jess closed the bedroom door behind her and pressed her head against it. *It wasn't fair. This was too much for any child to go through.* "I'm fine, Mom." She heard him call out on the other side of the door. "You can go away now."

Jess smiled a knowing smile. She stayed that way with her head pressed against the door until she heard his computer power up and with it, the steady drum of fingers hitting keys, and then she retreated to the comfort of her office and Myles's arms.

~

Just as summer turned into fall with the next several months came change and a steady stream of improvement around the Clemens's estate. Jess stayed clean, attended regular Narcotics Anonymous meetings, and volunteered at Cat's school.

Myles managed the heavy lifting around the property and helped maintain a sense of normalcy in Spencer's absence. He encouraged Jess to visit her father, and one day, in early November, she finally did.

Early one morning, they'd been wrapped up in each other and it was almost dawn. The light was just peeking through the curtains when he'd suggested it out of the blue. Jess still played the game of sneaking out of the main house once the kids had fallen asleep and hurrying off to her office above the barn, where she'd climb in bed with Myles. They'd make love and talk, often until dawn on the many nights neither of them could sleep. And there were many of those.

"Why don't you visit your father?" he'd asked.

Jess inhaled sharply, she hadn't expected the question. "It's complicated. But for starters, he doesn't even know who I am. I guess I just don't want to remember him that way..."

"Hmm. I'm sure there's a lot you still want to say to him though, right?"

She shrugged. "I haven't really thought about it."

He sighed. "Sure you have. The thing is, now's the time to say it, Jessica. Once a person's gone, they're gone, and you don't get a second chance. They're really gone, and all you're left with is the emptiness and the things you didn't say."

"He probably wouldn't understand what I was saying anyway."

"But you would, Jess. And really, that's what will comfort you once he's gone."

She snuggled in closer. "I'll think about it…"

"The sun's coming up."

She slowly untangled herself from him and started to get up. "Yeah, I'd better get back." She squinted trying to spot her clothes on the floor through the dim glow of the candlelight. "We're practically vampires living this way…"

He pulled her back down and wrapped his arms around her. "Yeah, well, you should know, vampire or not, being here with you has been some of the best days of my life."

Jess lifted her head and studied his face. "Whoa, Mr. Serious. Where's Myles and what did you do with him?"

He playfully bit her neck. "He's evolving. I think he's figuring out that maybe he likes the light after all."

THE FOLLOWING MORNING, JESS STOOD IN THE DOORWAY OF her father's room at the retirement community. She stood there for a few minutes, watching him reading the newspaper and thought back over her childhood and all of the mornings she'd watched him do the same thing. Countless mornings. Countless mornings that she could've said all that she had wanted to say, mornings where he would have known who she was and would've responded appropriately. But this was now. And this was not one of those mornings.

He looked up and then met her eye. "Did you bring my breakfast?"

Jess looked around before figuring out that it was her he was speaking to. "No, Daddy. It's me, Jessica."

"I want my breakfast. It's eight-thirty. No one brought me my breakfast."

She looked out into the hallway and back at him. "Oh. Okay. I'll check."

He eyed her suspiciously. "Who are you? Where's Dorothy?"

"It's me, Daddy."

Jess watched him study her face and try to connect the dots. "I don't have a daughter," he finally said, shaking his head.

She crossed the room and sat down on his bed opposite the recliner he was in. "I see. Well… I just came to sit with you."

"Sit. For what?"

She thought for a moment and let the words come. "You see, I'm in some trouble and you look like just the man to help me out."

He considered her statement briefly. "I can't help you out. I haven't even had my breakfast yet."

Jess laughed. *There was the man she knew. She'd hoped that a part of him was in there somewhere. And there he was.*

His expression grew concerned. "What sort of trouble are you in?"

She exhaled slowly. "My life has unraveled. My husband is in jail for attempting to murder me and for embezzlement. I nearly drank myself to death and my father doesn't even know who I am."

"That doesn't sound right. Why would anyone want to murder you?"

"For money," she whispered.

He shook his head in understanding as though she'd just let him in on a secret, which no one else in the world knew. "It's always about money. Well, good. I'm glad they caught the bastard."

Jess laughed. "How are you, Daddy?" she asked slipping.

"I think you're confused, young lady." He moved his head to the side attempting to look outside into the hallway and lowered his voice. "I think you wandered into the wrong room."

"Maybe so. But look… do you think that we could pretend for a little while… because the thing is, I could really use an ear right now."

He stuck his bottom lip out and pondered her question for a second. "All right."

"I love you, Daddy," she started and paused before continuing. "And I'm so sorry that I haven't visited in a while. It's just hard for me. But I miss you. I miss you so much." She wept, not taking her eyes off his.

He reached over and patted her knee almost childlike. "Oh, that's all right, young lady. You can come here anytime and we can play pretend, even before I've had my breakfast. It's fine, just so long as you don't cry."

She wiped her nose with the back of her hand. He passed her a tissue from his bedside table. "You've always been the best father. And the truth is, I'm not sure any man could ever live up to you. Maybe that was part of the problem, I realize in hindsight. But you know what… I think I finally found one that comes close."

He looked startled. "It's not that murdering son of a bitch, is it?"

Jess laughed hard then recovered. She shook her head. "No."

"I've never heard a story so crazy in all my life. You should write a book about that one. They'd probably make it into a movie. It just seems unreal."

Jess cocked her head to the side and smiled. "You don't say."

CHAPTER TWENTY-FOUR

Myles had spent so much of the last six months working to figure out and fix Jessica's problems that he'd neglected his own. In many ways, he welcomed this because it helped to take his mind off all that troubled him. It was easy, he found, to avoid dealing with your own issues when you were so engrossed in someone else's issues. And as a SEAL, it was what he knew. His experience taught him the necessity of intense focus.

He'd had one of the best summers of his life with Jess and her kids. It was nice to be regarded as somewhat of a father figure again, and God knows those kids needed it. He was glad to be with them. It felt good to be needed, and he was finally in a place that felt like the closest thing to 'home' that he'd known in a very long time. So much so that when his Commander contacted him late that summer and asked him to consider reenlisting, Myles told him that he was needed where he was and that he was happy there. Even still, the phone call and the mission that beckoned planted a seed in him that he couldn't stop from growing.

And admittedly, now that the intensity of saving

Jessica from herself was winding down, he found himself growing restless. He was trained to be a soldier. The ease and contentment of day-to-day family life wasn't something he was used to. Long story short, he wasn't sure he was ready for it. Or that he'd ever be ready, if he were being honest. He faced addictions of his own, and for better or worse, he still felt, and perhaps always would feel a deep sense of commitment to his team-mates. They were his brothers, and he missed the cama-raderie more than he thought possible. Not to mention, he craved the adrenaline that life in the military provided.

He was fairly certain he'd finally found his ex-wife and he'd meant to pay her a visit. There were still things left unsaid, but the time never seemed right to get away. *Soon. He would go soon.* He found himself thinking about this as he stood watching Jess accept her six-month sobriety chip from Narcotics Anonymous.

Watching her up on stage, he felt a deep sense of pride well up within him. Six months down, a lifetime to go, but he'd witnessed her strength grow over the past six months in ways that were immeasurable. She'd become a great workout partner, she was writing again, and most importantly, she was a better mother than he'd ever guessed she could be. Watching her parent was fascinating to him. She was tough and yet gentle in all the ways that mattered. And still, there was an uneasiness he couldn't shake.

In mid-November, when Jessica's mother offered to take the kids for the weekend, Myles suggested to Jess that they head to the coast. A part of him missed the simplicity of the beach house. Mostly, he missed being alone with her. And though he would probably never admit it willingly, maybe a part of him even missed her needing him the way she once did.

THEY PULLED UP TO THE HOUSE AS THE SUN HAD ALREADY begun sinking low in the sky. Jess immediately ran for the beach. Though Jess told him it could wait, Myles knew better and unloaded their things before he joined her out near the water. He stood there waiting for her to turn back. The wind had kicked up a bit and the water was choppy. A storm was coming. "Let's take a walk," she called over her shoulder and took off already several paces in front of him.

He eyed the black clouds rolling in. "We probably shouldn't go far."

Jess turned around and followed his gaze toward the sky. "It's just a stray shower coming in. It won't be too bad."

He knew better. Myles shrugged and jogged a few paces ahead of her. "Fine. Let's go. There's something I want to talk to you about anyway…"

She passed him. "Now?"

Myles stopped mid-stride and looked around at the empty beach. "It's as good a time as any."

"Maybe it is… but I don't know. I just have a lot on my mind right now. Can it wait?"

He furrowed his brow but recovered quickly. "Is there another choice?"

Jess stopped and bent over. She exhaled as loudly as she could. "Okay. You're right. I'm sorry… let's hear it."

He kept walking before stopping and turning around. "Nah, no worries. It can wait. It's really not that important, anyway. How's the writing coming?"

"It's not."

"I went over your timeline. I left you my notes in the drawer, just in case it helps."

She stuck out her bottom lip just a tad. "That was thoughtful of you."

Myles watched the big raindrops begin to fall. He could smell the heavy rain coming. "It's no big deal. We should turn back."

"Just a little while longer. I love the rain."

He looked up at the sky. It was turning darker by the second. "It's not the rain I'm worried about. You don't want to get caught in a storm like this, Jess."

"Maybe I do."

He hesitated. "I don't think you realize what you're in for."

She sat down in the sand and dug her feet in. "If you want to go Myles, just go."

He wasn't going to leave her there. He wasn't that kind of guy. And maybe she wasn't that kind of girl. Because she'd known, she'd seen right through him, and she'd called him out on it—and to her credit, she'd given him the option. But it wasn't completely lost on him that she hadn't asked him to stay either.

THEY SAT IN STUBBORN SILENCE AS THE STORM PICKED UP steam. Jess sat watching the light show in the sky while he watched her. Finally, with the rain beating down on them, for no apparent reason, she stood up. Myles followed suit. He waited for her to give in while they stood there in an unspoken standoff facing one another until a roll of thunder sounded, startling them both. Jess turned and made a run for it and he followed close behind. The sky lit up and the thunder sounded all around as buckets of rain poured from the sky. He counted the distance between the flash and the boom and as the gap closed, he picked up speed a little, but found Jess unable to keep up. She stopped and doubled over.

Myles turned back and bent down in front of her. "Climb on."

"You are not carrying me!"

"I'm not leaving you, either. And *I* want to get out of this weather. It's getting cold out. And, the way I see it, we don't have many options. Don't be stubborn now, Jessica. This isn't the time."

Jess eyed him, her expression pained. After a few seconds, she relented and climbed on his back. He lifted her up and through the thunder and the rain, he heard the words he hadn't expected would come so soon, if at all. "Don't worry about it. I understand."

She understood. Myles felt his breath catch. A part of him wanted to stop then and there, put her down, and explain where he was coming from. But they were in the thick of the storm, and the only thing Myles could focus on was what he'd been trained to do, and that was to get back to safety. So, instead he sucked in as much air as he could manage and made for the cottage.

Unsure what to say and whether or not to say anything at all, Myles handed Jess a towel he'd left on the counter and then grabbed another for himself. He turned and watched the rain pound against the glass. "That's some storm rolling in."

When she didn't respond, he turned to find her glaring at him. She toweled off her hair and wrung it out before she walked over to him and pressed her wet body against his. Her expression was unreadable, which was almost never the case anymore. "Make love to me," she said with her eyes on his.

Myles studied her face and smoothed her wet hair away

from it. Then he slowly peeled her out of her clothes and stripped out of his until they were standing in the middle of the living room naked, staring at one another in silence. "Have you forgotten what to do?" she finally asked, her expression confused.

Myles shook his head. "No."

"Then what are you waiting for?"

"There's no need to rush this. Maybe I just want to take you all in."

Jess gazed at the floor and then met his eye again, refusing to ignore the elephant in the room. "How long do I have before you go?"

Myles placed his finger to her lips. "We don't have to decide that now."

"Unless one of us already has."

He lowered his tone. "I said we'll talk about it later."

To his surprise, she didn't push back. And, he found this both a blessing and a curse.

CHAPTER TWENTY-FIVE

M yles watched the rise and fall of her chest as she slept. *Leaving her was going to hurt like hell.* But he was made for leaving. It's what he knew. One thing about military life was that there was no way of making everyone happy. If he stayed, neither of them would be happy, but if he went, they at least stood a chance apart. She wouldn't ask him to stay, he realized. She wasn't that kind of woman.

He was being called toward something bigger. His expertise being called for elsewhere, his brothers needed him back in the Navy. He had a duty and it was becoming more and more clear that it was in the military. So, while it wasn't an easy decision, it was at least clear-cut. You go where you're needed, and Myles knew as well as anybody that place was no longer where he was. Jessica would be fine. The kids would be fine. It was win-win, really. He wasn't cut out for family life and never had been. Even the small part of him that wanted to stay knew that if he listened, they'd ultimately all lose.

She stirred, opening her eyes. "Hey."

"Hey."

Light poured in and filled the room, causing her to squint. "What time is it? Did you sleep?"

"It's six-thirty. A little..."

Jess frowned. "That means no."

He smiled faintly.

"Why didn't you wake me?"

"You looked peaceful."

She swallowed. "So are we going to talk about this?"

"We're talking..."

"When do you leave?"

"After Christmas."

Jess nodded. "Wow. That's right around the corner."

She wasn't going to make this easy. "How did you know?

"I don't know. Lucky guess..."

He pinched the bridge of his nose and exhaled. "I'm sorry, Jessica."

"There's nothing to be sorry about. I knew who you were when we started this. I didn't exactly take you for a family man, Myles." *The way she said his name killed him.* " Plus I have a lot going on with the kids, the divorce, and the upcoming trial. That's enough to keep me busy for another lifetime."

"I know you're hurt..."

"Disappointed, more than anything," she whispered, not missing a beat.

"Yeah." He forced a smile. "But you'll move on. You're a smart, incredible, beautiful woman. You'll do all right for yourself..."

Her eyes welled up and she swallowed hard. "And you?"

Myles thought carefully searching for the most appropriate response, all the while knowing he was about to tell the first lie he'd told in quite some time. "I'll be fine. I'm a soldier through and through. I was made for this."

~

Jess watched him squirm. She wanted to push back, to be stubborn—to argue with him the way only she could. She wanted to hate him or pretend that she was indifferent, but to her dismay, she was stuck somewhere between love and understanding instead.

She scooted into him, buried her head into his chest, and thought back to the first time she'd seen his face back in that barn. She remembered how she wanted to hate him then with his smug grin, and in that moment realized that she could no more hate him now than she could that first night she spent with him. He'd been right about her back then, and he was right sitting in front of her now. She was a fighter. She would make it through. He wasn't the staying kind—that much she knew from the get-go. And it had always been just a matter of time before he proved it to her.

Jess wanted to say all of this, to tell him to go, to get out now before it had the chance to hurt any more. She wanted to beg him to stay—but the only words that came were ones that made sense. She snuggled into his lap and let them slip off her tongue. "It's okay. You know where to find me when you get back."

He stared at her for a moment. "You don't have to wait for me, Jessica. I'm not asking you to do that."

"I know you aren't. But what else *can* I do?"

"Move on."

She sighed. "Oh, Myles. If I had any chance at that, I never would've started this to begin with. Love is love. It's not the sort of thing you can just turn on and turn off."

He wrapped a strand of her hair around his finger and tugged gently. "You don't understand what you're saying. You don't know how it is."

"So."

"So, don't make promises you can't keep."

'Promises?" She smiled. "Who said anything about promises, Mr. Serious?"

"All kidding aside, I really don't want you to put your life on hold, Jessica."

"Maybe not, but you haven't considered one thing."

"Oh? What's that?"

Jess leaned up and pulled his head down as close as she could manage. She searched his eyes until she got the response she wanted. "I don't have a choice. I'm in love with you."

"WHAT SHOULD I TELL THE KIDS?" SHE ASKED LATER THAT night over dinner.

Myles eyed her in the candlelight and his heart hurt. "Tell them I didn't have a choice."

She cocked her head to the side. "I thought you said you never lie..."

"Well, technically, it would be *you* lying. As for me, I only lie when it really, really counts."

"And this counts?" *Anger was seeping in.*

"They're kids, Jessica. They can't handle the truth in every situation life throws at them."

"What is the truth exactly?"

He glared at her as he chewed the bite he was working on and took his time before swallowing. "The truth is that I'm a SEAL. I've spent a good portion of my life in the Navy. It's a large part of who I am. And anyone in my life needs to understand that."

Jess threw her fork down. "At what point do those who love you become more important than that part of your life?"

"Your argument is weak, Jessica. I wouldn't try that one with me."

"And why would that be? It's a valid question."

"Because everything I do out there in the field *is* for those I love. What do you think keeps us going? It's not the pay— I'll tell you that. I've seen things you couldn't have horrible enough nightmares to rival. So don't tell me that I'm reenlisting because I don't care. That's bullshit. And I won't have it."

She picked up her fork as the tears spilled down her cheeks and pushed the food around her plate. "I don't know what you want me to say."

"You say that you'll either wait for me or you won't. It's pretty simple. And there are no expectations, Jessica. If it doesn't work for you, just say so. I'll be fine."

"Will you be hurt?"

He shook his head. "Disappointed."

CHAPTER TWENTY-SIX

"What do you get a girl who has everything?" Myles asked in the darkness of the night.

Jess smiled and pressed her face against his naked chest. "I have everything I want right here, right now, in this moment."

"But Christmas is kind of a big deal, or so, I hear. My mom always worked on Christmas and we didn't have much so… I'm sort of flying blind here."

She squeezed him. "Oh, you have no idea. I'm going to make this the best Christmas ever. Big tree, lots of lights—all of it. It's how I've always done it, but this year will be even bigger! You haven't lived until you've spent Christmas at our house."

He laughed. "I guess not."

Myles felt her mood shift. "You won't be back yet this time next year, will you?"

"No. It's an eighteen-month deployment. That's all I'm committed to…"

"And after that?"

He inhaled. "And after that we'll see. I care about you,

Jessica. You know that. But as for much more than that, I'm not sure what else I can offer."

She walked her fingers down the length of his chest and back up again. "It's enough, Myles. I'll miss you, sure, but I miss the pills, too. And if I can live without them, then I can live without you... for a while at least."

"I'm afraid you're going to have to."

"Okay," she said sitting up. "We don't need to beat a dead horse. I get it. I know you need reassurance that I'll wait. Even if you're not willing to admit it. That's fine. But I said I'll wait for you and I will. I just need to hear you say that you want me to."

He took her hand in his, grabbed her chin, looking directly into her eyes. "I'm not sure that anyone has ever really known me the way you do. You understand things about me that half of the time I don't even understand about myself. I want you to wait. I want to spend the rest of my life with you. I want you to be mine and mine alone. I can't imagine anyone else holding you this way. Is that what you want to hear? Because it's the truth. The selfish fucking truth. But the truth nonetheless."

"Love is selfish, Myles. It just is."

"I don't want to be selfish. I don't want to ask you to wait because I know it's not fair to you. You deserve someone who's going to be around. You deserve better."

"And you deserve someone who will wait. Is that what you want to hear?"

He saw the recognition in her eyes. "Maybe it is."

"Good then, it's settled. We have eighteen months to figure out how to be the best at what the other deserves."

He lifted her hand and gave it a firm shake. "You have yourself a deal."

She smiled and then he pushed her backward on the bed and made love to her in a way neither of them would soon forget. He realized that night that there are a million ways to say I love you. And at least half of them don't require words at all.

THAT CHRISTMAS WAS THE BEST OF HIS LIFE, JUST AS SHE'D promised. The four of them, he Jess and the kids, went out to an old tree farm in the country and cut down their own tree. Jess tried to show him the opulence of her lifestyle while he showed her the simplicity of his. They made a game of it, seeing who could shock the other. She insisted he attend fancy parties with the Hartmans and he insisted on building a fire and watching old holiday movies around it with hot cocoa. Surprisingly, he found himself happy either way, as long as he was with her. Being here with her this way, felt like home. The only home he'd really ever known.

His Christmas gift to her was almost complete even though finding time for it required additional stealth on his part. He'd gotten Jonathan a camera because God knew the boy needed to get out into the world and out from behind his computer. Metaphorically, he wanted him to try seeing things from a different point of view and starting behind the lens wouldn't hurt. For Kit Cat, he'd gotten her ballet slippers and a year's worth of lessons because she incessantly talked about being a ballerina and he knew she'd be a natural. There was something special about the way she lit up a room —much like her mother did, without either knowing it or trying. There was a presence they both possessed and Myles wanted to bottle it up and take it with him.

Christmas came and went with a level of chaos like he'd never seen. He'd secretly arranged to have Jess's father brought to the house for Christmas dinner and Myles found himself with an unfamiliar feeling—a severe case of nerves.

He wanted everything to go just perfectly and thankfully, it did. Jess had been so surprised that tears welled up in her eyes.

He gave the kids their gifts, which they seemed to enjoy, but true to their nature, they were out the door, off to the next thing. Once everyone had gone, he decided it was time for Jess's actual gift. He blindfolded her, put her into the mule, and drove her to the barn.

"Where are you taking me?" she'd asked.

He smiled even though she couldn't see it. "To the place where it all started."

He pulled up, turned off the ignition, and led her in by the hand. "Okay. Here. Stop. Sit…"

Jess did as he said and took a seat. He removed the blindfold and watched as she let her eyes adjust. She looked around confused.

"You're sitting on it."

She stood and eyed the chair.

"You got me a chair?"

"No. I made you a chair. I dismantled that old table I found you standing on and used it to make something a little more useful."

Her eyes grew wide and she ran her fingers over it. "Wow. It's beautiful. I had no idea you had this kind of talent."

"It's a writing chair, Jessica. To go upstairs, in your office. I want you to promise me something…"

She swallowed.

"Promise me that you'll wait. This is me… manning up and asking you outright. And that while you wait, I'm asking you to finish your book."

She studied his face. "I promise I'll wait. But that book was just fluff—it was just something I liked to do in my spare time, once upon a time."

"That book is a good part of why I'm in love with you.

You have a gift, Jessica. A way with words, like nothing I've ever seen."

She smiled.

"And, of course, I'm going to need something to read while I'm away. So… I want you to promise that you'll write not just *to* me, but for me."

Jess exhaled slowly. "Fine. If you insist."

Myles nodded. "Good. Then there's just one more thing. Wait here."

She took a seat in the chair and watched him disappear around the corner.

He reappeared with a puppy flanking his side. "Jessica, meet Romeo. Romeo, Jessica."

The black lab pup sauntered up to Jess and began licking her hands. "You got me a dog?"

"Not just a dog. Loyalty."

She wasn't convinced. "Loyalty, huh?" Jess rubbed his head as he chewed on her fingers. "Well, he sure is cute nonetheless."

"Romeo, come." She watched as the dog followed his command. He pointed his finger at the pup. "Romeo, sit." The pup sat and eyed him expectantly and then eyed Jess.

Myles walked over to where she was sitting. "Romeo, heel." The dog followed. "Lay down." The pup rested at her feet.

"See, he's loyal *and* trained. I've been working with him for weeks…"

Jess grinned, stood, and wrapped her arms around his neck. The puppy barked. "The kids are going to be thrilled. I can't believe you've had him hidden in here this entire time…"

"I wanted you to have a companion in my absence. Plus, every great writer needs a dog."

"I think you mean a cat. I think most writers have cats."

He kissed her forehead, rubbed her shoulders to warm her up, and then shrugged. "Same difference."

She rested her head on his shoulder. "I'm going to miss you so much."

"I'm going to miss you, too." He pulled back and met her gaze head on. "Merry Christmas, Jessica. I hope you're happy."

Jess wrapped her arms around him a little tighter. "The happiest."

~

CHAPTER TWENTY-SEVEN

M yles shipped out two days after Christmas. Letting him go was perhaps the hardest thing she'd ever done. More so than recovering from the accident and even more so than getting clean. It was like a piece of her went missing, and she in turn spent the next two months practically in her pajamas. Of course, she took care of the kids and the puppy, but for the most part, when they didn't need her attention, Jess spent most of her time alone.

Until one day in late February, Addison paid her a visit. Addison arrived as usual dressed to the nines.

"What in bloody hell is wrong with you?" she'd demanded. "You know what you need, Jessica?"

Jess considered her friend standing there and how much she adored her. "A man who doesn't leave?"

Addison put her hand on her hip. "No. A man who wants to come back. Myles tells me that you guys Skype regularly…"

"Yeah. But it's not the same."

"He says he's worried about you, Jessica."

"He said that?"

"Yes. And it's not good."

"Why not? I worry about him…"

"It's not good because he's worried for all of the wrong reasons… Don't you think he has enough to worry about out there without you looking like hell frozen over? It's time to pull yourself together. Make him excited to come home, Jess. Stop moping around. It's not doing yourself or anyone else any good."

"I'm not moping around… I've been writing."

Addison narrowed her gaze. "Writing what?"

"A book?"

She stuck her bottom lip out and nodded slowly. "Well, that's good. What's it about?"

"It's about you, actually."

"Me?"

Jess grinned. "Yeah… your life story."

"What? Addison cocked her head and then frowned. Why?"

"I don't know… it's interesting."

"You hate the choices I made. You were so angry at me for so long."

"I do not. And I wasn't exactly angry…"

Addison placed her hand on her hip and waited Jess out.

"Fine. I was a little angry. But that was before…"

"And this is now?"

Jess smiled a smile that lit up her entire face. *There were only a few people who could make her smile like that.* "Yes."

Addie considered her for a moment. "Get dressed. We're going out."

"Where to?"

She shrugged as if it were the most irrelevant question in the world. "I don't know… does it matter? Shopping probably. And you could use some hair color…"

Jess smiled and stood up. *She'd missed her 'tell it like it is' friend.*

"Oh, and Jess…"

"Yeah?"

"Write your own damned story."

SHE AND MYLES DID SKYPE REGULARLY BUT AS TIME WENT ON, depending on where he was, which was information he could never give Jess, the Skype calls came more infrequently. So Jess would write to him instead. She'd send him her latest chapter and he'd send her notes on what he thought. When he informed her that he'd shared her story with some of his buddies and that they were all enjoying hearing it and wondering when the next chapter was coming, she wasn't exactly thrilled. However, as time went on, she enjoyed hearing what they thought via Myles and knowing that she was at least providing a sense of entertainment, if nothing else.

Myles emailed her often. In the hours often late at night that she missed him most, she'd take out his emails, always just like Myles, short and to the point, and read them over and over until she could fall asleep—always thinking of him.

To: JessicaClemens@addressredacted.com
From: MylesIngram@addressredacted.com
Subject: Let me count the ways…

Dear Jessica,

You know me. I'm often a man of few words, but I just

wanted to take the time today to tell you what I love
about you…

Most of the time people don't want to hear the hard stuff.
They want you to placate them, to cradle their fears—to
soothe them so that it's okay so that they can keep playing
small—or not play at all.

In other words, they're lazy.

But not you. You're a fighter.

And that's just one thing I love about you.

As of today, there are exactly eleven months and fourteen
days until I hold you in my arms again…

Love,
M

JESS WROTE BACK.

To: MylesIngram@addressredacted.com
From: JessicaClemens@addressredacted.com
Subject: RE: Let me count the ways…

Dear Myles,

Seeing your name pop up on my phone is like checking the
mail and finding a handmade card stuck between a big stack
of bills.

It's like Christmas morning.

And blowing out candles on my birthday cake… because, you
know, the wish.

In other words, it's really nice.

The kids are well. Cat had a great recital. Jonathan's photo-

graph of Romeo made it to the second round of the contest he entered. Speaking of Romeo—that dog, I swear. He broke through the fence again and chased the mailman down. He just wanted to play, but the mail guy didn't seem to think it was so funny. You should have seen his face when I caught up with them. I think I'm going to have to get one of those invisible fence things. I think he needs your training skill... your deep voice and presence. I miss it, too.
Be safe and hurry home.

Love,
Jess

To: JessicaClemens@addressredacted.com
From: MylesIngram@addressredacted.com
Subject: How Much Do I Miss You?

Dear Jess,

You may be asking yourself how much I miss you...
In that case, or any other, I just want to take the time today to tell you that I miss you so much that I look for you in places you couldn't possibly be. You're in every sunrise, every sunset, in everything beautiful.
The past eight months have been the longest ten years of my life.
I won't feel whole until we're together again.
As of today, there are exactly ten months and three days until I hold you in my arms again...

Love,
M

P.S. Please ask Jonathan if he received my emails. I haven't heard from him in several weeks. Give Cat my love and tell her I loved the video. She is an amazing dancer, Jess. Tell her I'm sending something off for her this week.

To: MylesIngram@addressredacted.com
From: JessicaClemens@addressredacted.com
Subject: RE: How Much Do I Miss You?

Dear Myles,

Attached is the next chapter. I'm almost finished. How crazy is that?
Romeo is doing well. He got into something dead and smelled wretched the other day, and I had to bathe him myself. It was an experience for us both. You were right. He is a good companion.
As for Jonathan, no need to worry. There's a girl and let's just say that's where the majority of his time is going. He said he sent you a photo of the two of them...
And remember how worried I was that he'd never get out from behind that computer? Well, I hadn't factored girls into that equation.
Silly me.
Be safe and hurry home.

Love,
Jess

P.S. Cat received the doll and she was thrilled. It's beautiful, Myles. Really. Thank you for being so great to them. You have no idea how much it means to me.

❧

In September, about nine months before Myles was scheduled to come home and while on a girl's weekend with Addison and some of her friends, Jess's phone rang. Myles's name lit up on the screen.

Jess couldn't swipe it fast enough. It had been almost three months since she'd heard his voice.

"Hello. Myles!"

"Hey, there." She could practically see the smile she heard in his voice.

"Oh, my gosh. It's so good to hear your voice. I miss you so much."

"I miss you, too. And I'm sorry that I haven't been able to call. We've been deployed... I'm back on base now, but I'm not sure for how long." He sighed.

Jess's voice caught. "You sound tired."

"I'm fine. Just missing you, that's all..."

"Addison and I are in San Francisco. She's fun and all... but I can't help wishing I were here with you..."

"Just nine more months. And then I'm out. I've decided that, for good this time. I'm getting older, Jess, and I'm not sure I can hack this life anymore, to tell you the truth. Plus, there's a girl back home that means the world to me."

"Wow. I wasn't sure I'd ever hear those words from you..."

"Yeah, well, I got the pictures you sent. You look beautiful. You always were. But whatever you're up to these days, it looks good on you."

"Addison got ahold of me. I've been working with her and her trainer."

"Tell her I said hello."

"Oh yeah... before I forget... did you get my email about my big news?"

"No. We haven't had computer access for a few weeks..."

Jess beamed. "My divorce was final last week."

He laughed. *God, he sounded so good.* "So, you're a free woman now, huh?"

"Something like that."

"That's great news. But, hey, listen... I gotta run. There's a line here and they're staring me down. I'll call again just as soon as I can, okay?"

"I love you, Myles."

"I love you, too..."

She would do anything if she could keep him on that phone, anything to not have to hang up. "All right... well, be safe."

"Hey, Jess..."

"Yeah?"

"I can't wait to make you mine."

IN NOVEMBER, RIGHT BEFORE THANKSGIVING, ON A DAY WHEN Jess was particularly missing him, she sent him this:

To: MylesIngram@addressredacted.com
From: JessicaClemens@addressredacted.com
Subject: Today, I'm not even going to pretend.

Dear Myles,

Is it bad that I want it to be raining where you are? That I want the weather to be gloomy—dark and gray, so maybe, just maybe, in hopes that you're as miserable there as I am here without you.

I look around at all of the happy families preparing for the holidays and I think back to this time last year, and I ache for you to be here. It literally hurts, Myles. I didn't even know missing someone could physically hurt. But it can.

Sometimes, on days when the weather is nice, I sit out in the garden and I play games with myself. I pretend that you're there in my office above the barn waiting for me... or that you're out working and I'm waiting for you. And sometimes, I swear I even see you there, coming around the bend. And just for a second, I can breathe easily again. Until I realize that it's not real and my heart sinks.

I die a thousand tiny deaths every time I play this game.

And yet I play.

Be safe and hurry home.

Love,

Jess

To: JessicaClemens@addressredacted.com
From: MylesIngram@addressredacted.com
Subject: RE: Today, I'm not even going to pretend.

Dear Jess,

I'm sorry it's taken me several days to get back with you. I hope you're in a better place now. It kills me that you're hurting. If I had known what I know now, I never would have come. I'm sorry for that, Jess. I'm sorry for putting you through this.

The truth is you were right. There comes a certain point where the people you love dictate where you want to be. And I want to be back in Texas, there with you, where I left my heart.

But the good news is that I'll be home soon.

As of today, there are exactly seven months and eighteen days until I hold you in my arms again…

Love,

M

∽

THREE DAYS BEFORE CHRISTMAS, JESS WAS IN HER OFFICE wrapping the last of the kids' gifts when there was a knock at the door. "Miss Jessica." *Dean.*

"Come in."

"There are some people here to see you, ma'am." Jess frowned. *He sounded out of breath.*

She looked over her shoulder. His expression was twisted. Jess exhaled and dropped the scissors. "I'm coming…"

She started for the stairs and stopped when she saw the uniforms. Her face fell and she shook her head slowly. Slowly, she made her way down the stairs, one by one.

She straightened her back. *No. No. No.* "Can I help you?"

"Are you Mrs. Clemens?"

She nodded.

"Mrs. Clemens, we regretfully inform you that Myles Ingram was killed in the line of duty yesterday."

Jess collapsed and all she remembers now were the wails that came from somewhere deep within her body, guttural screams, and then Dean catching her and the rocking back and forth, back and forth. There were other things that happened that afternoon. Like Romeo trying to attack the officers when the screaming began and him lying at Jess's side, his head in her lap. At some point, Addison arrived and her mother took the children. But she wouldn't remember any of that. She only recalled the screams, the sound of herself begging, pleading with anyone and everyone, for the words they'd uttered not to be true.

∽

CHAPTER TWENTY-EIGHT

The days and weeks that followed will always be remembered as somewhat of a blur. There were moments of extreme clarity, for example, when decisions needed to be made. Jess was informed via a letter that Myles had designated her as the person to make these decisions. Oddly enough, they'd never discussed this, but the more Jess considered it, the more she realized that, to her knowledge, there was no one else to make them.

She was told that his body was being flown back and was set to arrive within a few days, but was given little information on what to do other than that. Jess hadn't a clue what to do. She had no idea whether he would want to be buried or cremated, and if he wanted to be buried, where. She was hoping for answers and went so far as to have Addison try to find his ex-wife, figuring maybe she knew and also to figure out where his daughter was buried, as this is where she figured he'd want to be.

The thing that happens when someone dies, Jess found, is that you think you'll have all of this time to process it, but instead, there's such a whirlwind of things that are happening around you and things that need to be taken care of that there isn't time to deal with anything other than the task at hand.

It was too bad that Jess had spent so much time fretting over what to do because had she only known what would arrive three days later, she certainly could have and would have saved herself a ton of worry. Jess had been out walking Romeo around their property line when a UPS truck stopped to deliver a package. Jess signed for the box. She hadn't been expecting anything, but once she saw the outside of the brown box, she knew.

She regarded the box as though maybe it contained a bomb or anthrax. She studied it. Her name and address were neatly written in Myles's handwriting, and for a second, it was like nothing had happened at all—that he was still simply away, making his way back to her, a little more day by day. And when she looked at it like that, she considered that maybe it was true in some sense. Depending on what one believed about what happens after one dies, perhaps each day lived was one day closer to him in death. It was this thought that would carry her through in the months to come.

Jess immediately took the package back to her office and opened it. As she gently shook the contents out, she realized that the box held most of Myles's personal belongings. She laid them out, one by one, on the bed where they'd spent so much time. Then she sat down on that bed, placed her head in her hands, and wept. When the tears quit falling, she lay down, wrapped herself in a t-shirt she'd so often remembered him wearing, and sobbed herself to sleep.

It was near dusk when she finally awoke to Romeo nudging her. *He needed to go out.* Jess opened the door to let him out and then eyed the contents that were splayed out on the bed once more before picking up the white envelope with her name written across it. She ran her fingers over it as she imagined where he was and what his expression might have been when he'd written it. The letters of her name were displayed in that same familiar handwriting that for so long had made her heart leap whenever she saw it. Now it was simply a heavy reminder of all that would be forever missing. She took a deep breath and heard his voice ring in her ear. *Open it, Jessica. What are you waiting for?*

Jess carefully opened the envelope and removed the letter. She unfolded it, sat down in the chair Myles had made for her, and read the final words he'd written to her.

Dear Jessica,

They tell us to write these letters in the event of our death, and I've always found it quite silly to write down all of the things that one might never have to say. But then I met you. And to tell you the truth, there's still so much I want to say to you that I don't know how one letter could possibly ever contain it all. But then again, you know me. I've never been exactly heavy on the emotion, so while I'd like to write you a novel—hell, a series for that matter —sadly, this will have to be enough.

First things first, on the business side of death, there are a few things you need to take care of—I want to be cremated and half of my ashes buried next to my daughter. The information and address can be found on the back of this letter. As for the other half, I'd like for you to spread them at the beach house—when you are ready. Just don't wait too long, Jess, you need to move on. I know your heart, and I don't want you to be one of those people who hang on *too* long. I want you to let me go and know that by you going on, that's where you'll find me. No more than three months, okay?

I have money in an account that you are the beneficiary of.

The details are also on the back of this letter. I want you to make that money mean something. Every penny you ever paid me is in that account. I had planned to give it all back, anyway. Once I fell in love with you, I never wanted a dime for working for you. I want you to know that I would have done it for free, and I guess in a sense I have—aside from the pain I caused you now, that is.

But speaking of that, you need to know I died doing what I loved. Military life is what I knew. It's what made me who I am. And the brothers I've come to know here mean more to me than anything aside from you and my daughter. So, first and foremost, know that I died a happy man. How many people get to say that, Jess? Well, I did. And that's really quite a beautiful thing. The Navy welcomed me when I had no one. It made me a man and it held me when I had nothing. I'm sure a huge part of you is and will be incredibly angry with me for going back in—now knowing the outcome. But I hope in time you will come to understand that I died being completely one hundred percent who I was meant to be. That said... I realize doing so has hurt you, and Jonathan and Cat. The three of you have been everything to me over the past year. Having the opportunity to meet you and become a part of your lives will forever remain one of the highlights of mine. Other than having Hailey, loving you will always be one of the best things I ever did. And no matter how much time goes by or how short our time was together—I want you to know that for me it was real.

What we shared was what I would call the pure kind of love, Jessica. We came together two broken people, and it was our shared brokenness that made that kind of love so rare, and for a little while, it made us whole. I've been a lot of places and seen a lot of things, and I will tell you there is nothing more beautiful than that.

Helping you get clean was one of the greatest accomplishments of my life. Now that I am gone, there is really only one choice you have to make, Jessica. Either, you can take what we had and expand on it or you can die right alongside with me. But know that if you do this, if you close yourself off, you are in essence letting the purity of what we had, and in a sense, our time together go to waste. Yes, our time was cut short. Yes, there should have been more—but if you care at all about me, you will promise me that you will not let it have been all for not.

I need my life to have meant something, beyond being a soldier who died serving his country. I need to go on in the world even though I'm not in it. And I know that you're creative, you'll figure out how to best make that happen. And most importantly, I trust that you won't let me down.

Finish the book, Jess. And then write ten more. Tell your stories. Tell mine. Tell the stories of millions who can't or won't tell them themselves. Your words are what have kept me going when I was out here in the dark, fighting—waiting another day just to be closer to where you are.

From the very beginning, your words were my light when I strained to see. Take your pain, take my pain, take the joy, take it all—and put it into words. That's how we go on, Jess. Just because I am gone doesn't mean that what we had has to die, too.

I trust that you'll keep going. You told me once that I saved your life, but I want you to know that, in many ways, you saved mine. You gave me hope when for so long I'd had none, hope that something amazing was waiting for me back home. Because *you* were my home. You gave me direction, a purpose beyond what I thought possible.

And I trust that you'll keep the promises you made to me in that silly little contract I wrote once upon a time. I trust that you know that even if you hadn't kept those promises—you know that I would have loved you anyway. It was always meant to be exactly as it was. Tell yourself that, Jessica. In the hard times, when you can't sleep, when you're missing me more than you ever thought possible. Tell yourself that and, one day, you might just find yourself surprised that you hear those words and feel joy. I never thought that anything good could ever come out of losing Hailey, but I was wrong, Jessica. There was you. And it was always meant to be the way it was.

Love,
M

P.S. Please give Jonathan and Kit Cat all my love and give them their letters when you feel the time is right. There is no rush. Trust your instinct. You are doing fine. You've always been stronger than you've given yourself credit for. I love you. And I know that you love me, too. If I had to go, and obviously, I did, there was nothing better than going knowing that.

~

EPILOGUE

The months following Myles's death were probably the most horrendous of Jess's life. Spencer's trial began exactly four months to the day, and the only time that Jess stepped foot in the courtroom was when it was her turn to testify. She hadn't wanted to testify for or against her husband, but in the end, relented as to further prove that she had no involvement in the mess that he'd created.

His lover testified that Spencer had planned her death for approximately six months prior to the time the accident took place. According to him, Spencer had outlined several ways of offing her, but ultimately, decided that a car accident was the least likely to get him busted. Looking back, Jess could connect the dots on things that were off during that time—more so than she did when she was living it. It's ironic to her how accurate the saying 'hindsight is twenty-twenty' actually is. According to his lover, her now ex-husband ran through several methods of taking her out including poisoning her. When Jess later thought back on it, she could remember a time when Spencer insisted on making her morning smoothies before her yoga class and how sick she'd gotten once or twice. And how after that, she refused them all together to his insistence that she wasn't getting the nutrients she required.

According to David Dewitt, the accident was orchestrated right down to the exact science of it and had been rehearsed several times. David testified that he was instructed to call Spencer's cell phone at midnight in order to allow him the opportunity to drop it—causing Jess to have to unbuckle and him to swerve to hit a tree. Apparently, he did not plan as far as her surviving, though somehow, by the grace of God, she did. There were a few doctors, and of course, Addison, who told the jury that while she was in the hospital in a coma he was a little more than insistent on removing her from life support in the days before she recovered enough to come out of it on her own.

In the end, Spencer pled not guilty, refusing all plea bargains, and received two life terms for attempted murder and embezzlement. Jess never did get a chance to discuss any of it with him. He denied her requests for visitation, but she did read a victim's statement during the sentencing phase of the trial to make her feelings known. In the beginning, he wrote to the kids a few times, but his correspondence faded as quickly as his early days in prison turned to years.

Jonathan is currently away at Cambridge and was a published author at the ripe old age of sixteen. Catherine is finishing her senior year in high school and would be off to The Ballet Department at Indiana University in the fall. They are the most brilliant of young adults. Jess possibly couldn't be more proud of where they are headed. Despite the trials and tribulations they faced, they are fighters, and her relationship with them is better than she could have ever imagined. There is an honesty and realness to it that perhaps wouldn't have surfaced any other way, in spite of the hard times.

Jess fulfilled Myles's wishes by taking his ashes to be buried next to his daughter Hailey. The other half, she spread in the ocean exactly three months to the day he died—she purposely waited as long as she possibly could, but made deadline according to the wishes in his letter. She even went a step further and hand delivered the letter he'd written to his ex-wife, if for no other reason than so she could convey the things to her that she knew Myles had always wanted to say—which summed up were— that he *had* really loved her and their daughter, and that he'd always wanted to be what she'd wanted him to be—and that he spent a lot of time being sorry that he wasn't.

As for Jess, personally, she did finish that novel, as well as many others. In the years that followed, she poured every ounce of heartache she possibly could into her work and it turned out, for the most part, well for her. She may not have realized it then but from the day he asked her to write it, it was always him she wrote to... then and every day since. Every single word written was written with him in mind. He was and always would be her ideal reader, so to speak—for he believed in her long before she believed in herself.

There were many days she sat and stared at the bend of her property and swore she saw him coming around it. There were times where she thought if she just focused hard enough, she could make it so and days where she was certain it was actually him she was seeing. In any case, she hopes she has done Myles proud. She hopes that she has honored him and his life and that through her maybe a piece of him has lived on in some way.

One year to the day of his death, Jess created a non-profit organization in his honor that provides soldiers returning to civilian life not only clothing but the necessities they would need to make the transition easier for them. She never forgot that conversation with Myles about burning Spencer's clothing—about all that was spoken and all that was left unsaid. There was a certain level of forgiveness and acceptance that he possessed that was like nothing she'd ever known. It has been her greatest hope that the foundation she created in his honor would carry that message forward.

About three years following his death, Jess was at a charity fundraiser when she ran into the man Myles had named as his father. Jess sauntered right up to him and asked him if he'd had any idea what he'd missed. She told him of his son and his life and the amazing man that he was, and judging by the look in his father's eyes as he stared back at her, she found some sense of closure in that deep down a part of him *had* understood. For it was the same look that she'd often seen written across his son's face, a look that she missed more than words could or would ever convey.

Ultimately, Jess owed Myles Ingram everything. He taught her how to love again—how to love herself, how to want more, how to demand it, and how to execute. He taught her to wait for that which was worth waiting for and to fight for what is worth fighting for. He taught her about sobriety, and discipline, about feeling pain, and learning to live with it and in spite of it. But most importantly, he taught her what real love is. And as much as she would have liked to find a love like that again, the truth is she never has. Maybe someday… she hasn't ruled it out…

The great lesson of Myles for Jess would always be that sometimes people come into our lives for reasons we may not understand at the time, but that these people end up changing the course of our lives—forever and for the better. And no matter how long they end up staying—whether it's for a long time or a very brief period, these people matter, and that honoring them and what they stood for is the most important work of one's life. His love taught her to keep going, for it is the only choice there is. It proved that pain, addiction, and ultimately, loss, as hard as it is to live with, and as bad as it sucks, has nothing on the power of love.

AFTERWORD

Dear Reader,

I hope you enjoyed reading my novel. Your engagement with my work means a great deal to me.

If it was your cup of tea, I'd be grateful if you'd consider leaving a review on Amazon.

Want to be the first to know when my next book is out? Sign up for my newsletter and never miss a release. (https://brit neyking.com/newsletter/)

Thank you for your support—it truly means a lot to me.

And now, enjoy a sneak peek of another one of my books…

Britney King
Austin, Texas
November 2024

ABOUT THE AUTHOR

Britney King lives in Texas with her family, two literary dogs, one ridiculous cat, and a partridge in a pear tree.

When she's not wrangling the things mentioned above, she writes psychological, domestic, and romantic thrillers.

You can find Britney online here:

Web: https://britneyking.com
Facebook: https://www.facebook.com/BritneyKingAuthor
TikTok: https://www.tiktok.com/@britneyking_
Instagram: https://www.instagram.com/britneyking_/
BookBub: https://www.bookbub.com/authors/britney-king
Goodreads: https://bit.ly/BritneyKingGoodreads
Newsletter: https://britneyking.com/newsletter/

Want to make sure you never miss a release? Sign up for Britney's newsletter: https://britneyking.com/newsletter/

ACKNOWLEDGMENTS

Many thanks to my family and friends for your support in my creative endeavors.

To the beta team, ARC team, and the bloggers, thank you for making this gig so much fun.

Last, but not least, thank you for reading my work. Thanks for making this dream of mine come true.

I appreciate you.

ALSO BY BRITNEY KING

Series

The Killer Series

Kill, Sleep, Repeat
Kill, Sleep, Repeat Volume II

The New Hope Series

The Social Affair / Book One
The Replacement Wife / Book Two
Speak of the Devil / Book Three
The New Hope Series Box Set

The Water Series

Water Under The Bridge / Book One
Dead In The Water / Book Two
Come Hell or High Water / Book Three
The Water Series Box Set

The Bedrock Series

Bedrock / Book One
Breaking Bedrock / Book Two
Beyond Bedrock / Book Three
The Bedrock Series Box Set

The With You Series

Somewhere With You / Book One
Anywhere With You / Book Two
The With You Series Box Set

SNEAK PEEK: HER

"After four, I quit counting. What's the point if you know it isn't going to stop?"

Sadie is jealous. Why wouldn't she be? Her life is falling apart. Meanwhile, her new neighbor is everything she is not.

Ann is perfect—the kind of woman everyone loves to hate-- and a best friend to die for. She hosts over-the-top dinner parties, takes parenting to an entirely different level, and makes ambition look sexy as hell.

Sadie learns quick: the best way to cure jealousy is to befriend it. She also learns there's more to her new friend than meets the eye. She's patient, she's kind, and possibly a serial killer.

It isn't until Ann's proclivities hit a little too close to home that Sadie has to ask herself how much she's willing to over- look in the name of getting what she wants.

Exquisitely paced, *Her* is an unnerving and electrifying psychological thriller about jealousy, passion, and the dangerous places desire can take you. Full of enough tension and twists to make even the most seasoned suspense reader break out in a cold sweat, it keeps you guessing until the very last page.

HER: A PSYCHOLOGICAL THRILLER

BRITNEY KING

COPYRIGHT

Hot Banana Press
Cover Design by Britney King LLC
Cover Image by Britney King LLC
Copy Editing by Librum Artis Editorial Service
Proofread by Proofreading by the Page

First Edition: 2019
ISBN 13: 9781797040912
ISBN 10: 97817970409

britneyking.com

This is not for you.

"The truth will set you free, but first it will piss you off." — Joe Klaas

PROLOGUE

Now

I wish someone had told me: worry is a waste of time. The real troubles of your life will be things that never even bothered to cross your mind.

Nine months, three days, and nineteen hours, I've lived down the street from her. If you really think about it, a person can do a lot in nine months. They can gestate a fetus and deliver it safely into the world, and they can also plant roots and create an entirely different life altogether. That's what she did.

Not that I realized it at the time, but in essence, that's what she helped me to do, too. What's good for the goose is good for the gander, as they say. Only she isn't a bird. She can't just fly away, the way she thinks she can.

She thinks she can migrate, start a new life elsewhere, someplace where she can be whatever she wants to be. But she's forgetting two things: wherever you go, there you are. Also, there are people like me.

When I moved to this boring, homogeneous, monotonous

little town, I did so with one intention and one intention only: to have a nice life. A quiet life.

That's not how it played out. Not even close.

First, it was good. And then it got bad before it got good again.

I met her and life changed.

What can I say? I got swept up in it. She makes it easy. Her, with her impractical shoes and her perpetually sunny nature. For me, she always has felt a bit like spring in the middle of winter. She was then, and still is to me now, just about the most wonderful thing in the world.

But there's something to be said for that. Something I hadn't realized at the start. It was a new experience for me, and I felt dizzy for a while. Like most things, dizziness fades. And then, it dawns on you, the relationship you have in your mind is profoundly different from the one you actually have.

Of course, it takes precious time before you figure this out. Only by then, it's too late. By then, desire has already taken you to the darkest edges of humanity. It's a special place in the deepest recesses of hell, let me tell you. That's when you realize what they say is true: Every love affair has its rituals—and you always kill what you love in the end.

On so many occasions, this could have taken a different route. She could have proven me wrong, and yet so many times she took exactly the route I predicted. We all make choices. She made hers. I made mine. Those choices have consequences. I'd like to think I've been lenient with her, far more lenient than I should have been.

So, that's how I've found myself here, at the end that's really a beginning. Here, in her kitchen, sitting at her bar, turning the knife over in my hands. All the while knowing that what awaits me upstairs will not be easy.

It's okay.

No one ever said revenge was easy. Just sweet. One of her

favorite sayings. She was wrong about a lot of things—me, for one—but *that*, well, that she was right about. Revenge is surprisingly sweet. It's clear in the steadiness of my breath, in the clarity that has washed over me. My hands don't even shake.

There are eleven steps to the top of the stairs. I've counted.

Her death will not be random. A crime of passion, they'll call it. Although it will not be done in the heat of the moment, the way one might suspect. No. This is a scene I've played out in my mind, hundreds, if not thousands, of times. I knew it wouldn't be easy. She is my friend, my only friend. She prefers it that way.

Yes, I am aware of how pathetic this sounds. I wish I knew how to make you understand. It's just…well, I've never been very good with words. That's her gift. Mine is asking questions. Maybe I should start there. Have you ever met someone you know is absolutely terrible for you but for whatever reason, combined with all the mysteries of the universe, you just can't help yourself? Well, for me, that person is her.

I can't help myself. She's black magic and at the same time the air I need to breathe. Which is why I was careful to prepare for any and all setbacks. Setbacks have always been our specialty.

I finish off my Danish, careful to savor it in the way that she would appreciate. Next, I slip off my shoes, and leave them neatly by the door, just as I have countless times before, on more pleasant visits.

To outsiders, her death will come as a shock. Obviously, not for long. I've accounted for this. Which is to say, I don't plan to stick around. Statistics show most victims know their perpetrators. Murder is astonishingly predictable. Since the beginning of time we've been sleeping, eating, having sex, and murdering each other. And not necessarily in that order.

Why no one ever sees these things coming is beyond me.

She really should have seen it coming.

Trust is a slippery thing though, isn't it? Intangible, I've come to find. It doesn't matter how smart your brain is. The heart is a different organ entirely. At least, this is the only logical explanation I can come up with as to why the truth so often remains elusive even when it's dangled right in front of us. It isn't logical at all. For so long, I thought if I just tried hard enough, I could make this work. There's a price for that kind of stupidity. And believe me, I paid it.

Now, it's her turn.

You live and you learn, I suppose. And let me tell you, I have learned…

At the top of the stairs, I will find her in her bed, third door to the right. By this time of night, she will be sleeping on her side, covers pulled halfway up. Her expression will be slack, but peaceful, for even in sleep women like her know only ease.

On the left side of the four-poster bed, is a nightstand. On top of the nightstand rests her Bible, the cell phone she'll never reach, a glass of water she'll never drink, the reading glasses she doesn't want anyone to know she needs.

I will attack from the right, stabbing her six times. I've mapped it out. Six stab wounds, one for each of the ways she has wronged me. In reality, it doesn't take that much to kill a person. She probably knows this better than anyone. And if not, just in case, I want to make sure.

READ MORE: https://books2read.com/her